RISE STRONG~ SHINE BRIGHT

Time to Shine Your Destiny

BERNICE BROWN

Rise Strong~ Shine Bright
Alice, Texas, 78333

Printed in the United States of America.
ISBN : 9798863203072
Cover design by Justin Brown
Proofreading by Alvalene Rogers

For more information, or to book an event, contact :
Email : lavandared.com
http://www.iamlavandared.com

"To All the Bethesda's,

While your given names might differ, know that each of you embodies the spirit of Bethesda inwardly. There is a unique resonance in the name Bethesda — a reminder of pools of healing, of solace, and of stories yet untold. This spirit, whether in name or essence, carries with it a legacy of strength and renewal.

It is no accident that many of you resonate with this spirit, and like the Bethesda of old, you too possess the power to overcome, to transform, and to offer solace. The world may at times overlook the deep reservoir of strength within you, mistaking your gentle waves for calm passivity. But remember, even the most tranquil waters run deep, and beneath your surface lies a force to be reckoned with.

May you always remember that life's challenges can transform into pillars of strength and perseverance. Rise, heal, and continue to be a beacon of hope for those around you. Because in your spirit lies a promise — a promise of renewal, transformation, and endless possibilities.

Never underestimate your innate power to influence and inspire the world with your brilliance.

GRATITUDE

To My God Be the Glory All the Things He Has Done For Me

CONTENTS

FOREWARD

Since coming to know my sister in Christ, Bernice Brown, several years ago, I know the Father lives and moves within her. I have never seen her faith waiver, as she has always shown herself to be steadfast, immovable, and unshaken in her faith, always trusting the Father's promises and continuously hoping in the Lord's ability to unmask raw diamonds in any negative situation.

After reading this awesome book, I was left wanting part 2. May true love reveal the need to be equally yoked and an extension of the Father's love, enhancing and propelling single women, becoming wives and mothers, deeper into God's divine will, being in the center of His perfect will, fulfilling your dreams, and ALWAYS looking to the Father for hope and direction.

This book is truly a reminder of a lesson I learned in *James 1:4: "Let perseverance finish its work so that you may be mature and complete, not lacking anything.*

May there be NOTHNG MISSING, NOTHING BROKEN in your life.......

Brenda Cuney

INTRODUCTION

In the tapestry of life, societal standards and expectations frequently have a strong influence on the decisions we make. During my early years, society made an uncompromising statement: women had to marry at a certain age or face being called "old maids." This unforgiving reputation hung over the heads of numerous young women, becoming a phantom that haunted every move they made. Many made commitments under the influence of fear or other circumstances, allowing society's clock to dictate their decisions rather than the natural rhythm of the heart.

The wisdom of Proverbs 18:22 states, "Whoso findeth a wife findeth a good thing, and obtaineth favour of the LORD." It emphasizes the profound idea that finding a life partner requires judgment and divine intervention. But what happens when impatience triumphs over faith?

Enter Bethesda's world, where she is a victim of societal rules. She finds herself connected to Daniel, a man suffering from the invisible chains of mental illness, unable to wait for destiny's hand. On the surface, their relationship looks normal, but behind the surface lies a chaotic tempest of control, sorrow, and darkness. Bethesda longs to be Daniel's saviour with all her love and compassion.

However, she soon realizes that her love, no matter how profound, cannot heal the demon that inhabits him. It's a demon that only he can face.

As you read through these pages, you might see snippets of your own story mirrored in theirs. The complexities of love, societal pressures, and internal battles are universal themes with which many struggle. Begin your journey and immerse yourself in the worlds of Daniel and Bethesda. Theirs is a narrative waiting to be told, one that will linger in your heart and stay with you long after the final word is read.

Bernice~

Proverbs 18:22

The man who finds a wife
Finds treasure and receives favor from the Lord.

Whoso seeks after such a wife and finds one.
Findeth a good one
It is from the Lord

And under His direction and guidance
In seeking, that he finds a good wife.
That wife that is intelligent, prudent, and industrious- a proper help
That is from the Lord

She is her husband's crown, jewel, his lover, his confident
She is like no other.

She is far beyond the price of pearls.
She is clothed in strength and capability, dignity, and valor.

She is wise, and she encourages her husband.
She is the heart of the home.
And to be married to one is to become one.
A wife aids her husband.
And make him delighted.
And they live together in peace, love, and harmony.

Nora Alaniz

CHAPTER 1

INTRIGUED HEARTS CONNECTS

*S*unlight shone through the stained-glass windows and lit the church with a soft glow that filled the seats with bright colors. It was a place of solace where souls searched for comfort and guidance. On this Sunday morning, amidst the hushed whispers and the faint scent of incense, a fateful encounter was about to unfold.

Bethesda stood in her normal spot midway through the church, scanning the crowd. She was stunning both in appearance and character. Her eyes were a blend of amazement and tenderness. A wave of brown curls framed her face, and her infectious smile could make anyone happy. She moved softly but precisely with confidence and ease as though everything she did had a purpose.

Because she was intelligent, humble, and always ready to listen and learn from others, she constantly challenged herself by trying new things, meeting new people, and reading books to gain a broader perspective. Her generosity and thoughtfulness extended to other's needs, making them feel important and understood. People found it easy to talk to her because she listened to them and seemed interested in what they had to say.

Even though she had many attractive traits, Bethesda stayed grounded and modest. She never tried to get notice or approval for herself. Instead, she focused on connecting with people and making a difference in their lives. Her honesty was a breath of fresh air in a world that often prizes superficiality.

Above all else, Bethesda had a strong will that kept her going as she tried to find happiness and satisfaction. She knew what she wanted out of life and wasn't afraid to take chances to get it. Her journey moved forward because she never stopped believing in the power of love and how important it was to follow her heart in finding Mr. Right.

Ultimately, Bethesda was a shining example of grace, kindness, and toughness. She left a lasting mark on the lives of everyone she met, and her presence showed how beautiful it can be to be one's true self. She had found comfort in the same routines and people at this church for many years. But today was not like other days. Her eyes darted around as she tried to locate the source of the unexplainable tugging at her emotions.

Then she finally spotted him.

A few rows back, a tall, strange young man stood with his arms crossed his chest holding what seemed like a Bible. His dark hair fell easily across his face, framing piercing blue eyes that seemed to hold a thousand stories. Immediately, she recognizes in him the divine incarnation of a strong, authoritative Man of God. Even though they just glanced at each other briefly, Bethesda's heart skipped a beat. It felt like a current ran between them, like they had been linked by looking at each other.

Her mind was racing with a whirlwind of feelings. Who was he? What was his name? Bethesda couldn't help but feel a peculiar attraction to this stranger believing that fate planned for them to meet on this day. Inward she heard a voice saying, "When a man finds a wife, he has found a treasure! For she is the gift of God to bring him joy and pleasure. She quickly rejected what she heard and came to her own conclusion that this feeling was not merely a coincidence.

As the service progressed, Bethesda's mind wandered. Her attention was torn between the prayers and hymns and the mysterious stranger seated several pews behind. She noticed that her interest in him grew more intense as her imagination and inquisitiveness flourished as time passed.

Again, she heard the voice speaking, "When a man finds a wife, he has found a treasure! For she is the gift of God to bring him joy and pleasure, and she ignores it.

But she didn't know how to approach him. How could she get

3

through the unseen wall that kept them apart? Bethesda thought about these questions while her heart was beating rapidly in her chest. She was always a shy, quiet girl who found comfort in her thoughts and the pages of her books. The thought of talking to a stranger, especially one who had made her feel so strongly, was exciting and scary.

As the last notes of the closing hymn faded away, Bethesda made a choice. The universe had brought them together for a particular purpose; she would take advantage of this chance. She mustered up the courage to approach the strange man, even though her heart was racing, and her hands were a little sweaty.

Her steps were timid at first, but as she got closer, a strange determination settled within her. She would not let fear keep her from discovering what fate had in store for them. Her glance never left him, her gaze drawn to him like a magnet.

When Bethesda finally stood in front of him, she couldn't breathe. She put out a shaky hand and introduced herself, but her voice showed her fear.

"My name is Bethesda. I couldn't help but notice you behind me."

The stranger's lips curled into a sweet smile, his eyes mirroring the intrigue in hers.

"Good day, Bethesda. "My name is Daniel," he said, his voice warm and friendly. "I couldn't help but take notice of you, too."

Bethesda understood at that moment that approaching him was the right decision. The church walls appeared to slip away as they traded stories and laughter, leaving only the two of them immersed in a world of their own creation. They had no idea that their meeting at the church would be the start of an unforgettable journey that would connect their lives in an unforeseen and meaningful way, ultimately demonstrating the endless possibilities of chance and the vastness of the unknown.

The extended talk between Daniel and Bethesda, as they moved toward the exit, was proof of their bond. They didn't want it to end, but reality called, and they realized it was time to say goodbye. They swapped phone numbers, vowing to continue their talk later that week. The spark in their eyes showed how excited they were to meet for the first time, and they both felt hopeful that this meeting could lead to something great. With a warm smile and a last wave, they walked out into the busy world, full of hope for what the future might bring.

They spent hours on the telephone when time did not permit them to see each other face to face. The more they chatted, the more they discovered about each other's backgrounds and values. Bethesda learns that Daniel grew up in a loving and caring home with his parents who instilled in him the importance of having a strong faith and attending church. But Daniel keeps this a secret. He enjoyed discussing only his mother and respected her commitment and faith, teaching him important lessons about kindness, forgiveness, and the power of prayer. Daniel said he learned to be truthful and considerate from his mother, who had a strong sense of right and wrong and was active in their community.

Bethesda noted Daniel's eyes seemed to brighten when he spoke of his mother and her faith. She finally realized that Daniel was a man with a strong spiritual commitment and could see how his background had influenced him to be honest and caring. This caused her to feel a great connection with him.

On the other hand, Daniel learned that Bethesda, life was rooted and grounded in spirituality and had a strong religious upbringing sought of comparable to his. Her parents were well known in ministry and held a solid belief in their faith which they instilled in Bethesda.

Bethesda and Daniel recognized how much they liked each other as they got to know each other better. They believed they shared the same aspirations and that their meeting was the beginning of something significant and were eager to see what would happen next. They were delighted to support each other's aspirations, confront life's hardships together, and grow closer by sharing values and beliefs after understanding they had much to learn from each other and that their paths had led them to this vital moment.

The two of them were on a journey of love, growth, and shared beliefs guided by their faith. They knew this was just the beginning of a beautiful story with many more scenes of happiness, strength, and growing closeness. They were ready to start their trip, knowing their solid foundation would help them get through any storms and celebrate the victories still to come.

CHAPTER 2

THE UNCONVENTIONAL UNION

*I*t had been months since Bethesda and Daniel had met by chance at the church. What began as a small spark had grown into a strong light of love and friendship. Over time, they found out they had similar goals, dreams, and beliefs, which made their relationship stronger. It was a fast-paced relationship that felt like it was meant to be from the start.

As Bethesda and Daniel's love for each other grew, they knew in their hearts that they were meant to be together for the rest of their lives. This causes them to take their love to the next level and get married because they loved each other and thought that their souls were connected. For them, it was a logical step.

However, as Bethesda excitedly shared the news with her family and friends, she couldn't help but notice a sense of apprehension in their reactions. They expressed concerns and doubts, their brows furrowed with worry. Bethesda's parents, who had always been her pillars of support, expressed genuine concern when she shared her intention to marry Daniel. Her mother's gentle voice was filled with worry as she questioned if it was the right time for such a significant commitment.

"Sweetheart, can you tell me more about how you and Daniel met?"

Bethesda smiled and said "Sure, Mom. We met at church a few months ago. I was attending a Sunday service, and when I saw him standing there with the Bible in his hands, I couldn't help but feel a connection. I believe that he was the answer to my prayer. And also, he reminded me so much of Dad, with his strong faith and kindness."

"Oh, really? That's interesting. What made you feel like he was the one you were praying for?"

"Well, you know how I've always admired the way you and Dad have such a strong spiritual bond. When I saw Daniel with his Bible, it gave me hope that we could have that too. He seemed genuine and sincere, just like Dad."

"It's wonderful to find someone who shares your values and beliefs. But, my dear, there's so much more to consider in a relationship. Have you had a chance to learn about his background, his dreams, and his plans for the future?"

"We've talked about some of those things, but I realize I haven't delved deep enough into those areas yet."

"It's essential to understand each other fully before making any decisions. Marriage is a beautiful commitment, but it requires a strong foundation of trust and understanding."

"Are you sure it's the right time, Bethesda?" her mother asked, her eyes searching for reassurance. "Marriage is lifelong commitment: it's not something you can easily walk out of. You must be prepared to stand by him through thick and thin. Maybe it's best to date him for a couple of years, to truly know if he's the right person for you."

Her father, too, chimed in with a hint of concern in his tone.

"My dear, we've always admired your ambition and career aspirations. Have you thought about how marriage might impact your plans? Balancing a career and raising children can be challenging. We have never made decisions for you once you became an adult, but I hope you'll take some time to pray about this, sweetheart."

"I understand, Dad. It's something I've been considering too. I know it won't be easy, but I believe with the right partner, we can support each other in our individual dreams."

"That's true, my dear. It's crucial to have open conversations about your goals and dreams, so you can both align your paths. When your mom and I first met, I was ready to sweep her off her feet and propose right away. But she insisted that we take our time and get to know each other better. It was during that time of courtship that we discovered things about each other, both good and challenging. We even had a brief time apart, but it helped us grow individually and brought us back together stronger than ever. Your mother was wise beyond her years. I didn't fully understand then, but I am grateful today that we took that time. It made our marriage so beautiful and meaningful."

Bethesda understood her family's concerns. They only wanted what was best for her, and their worries were born out of love and a desire to protect her from potential heartbreak. But in her heart, she knew that her connection with Daniel was different, that their love was genuine and deep.

With conviction in her voice, Bethesda replied, "I understand your concerns, and I appreciate your love and support. But Daniel and I have a connection that transcends time. We have shared dreams and values, and we believe in our love. I don't want to let fear or doubts hold us back from building a beautiful future together."

Even her friends didn't like the idea. They were worried about how quickly their relationship was moving, and they wondered if Bethesda was making a choice before fully thinking it through.

Bethesda's family and friends also noticed that as her friendship with Daniel grew, she cared less about helping other people. Bethesda used to spend a lot of time and energy being there for her friends and family, taking on the weight of their issues. They trusted her as a confidante because she really cared about what they had to say and could calm and understand them.

However, Bethesda only became increasingly concerned about bringing happiness to Daniel who had advised her to balance helping others and putting oneself first, with him as the focal point. He knew she was thoughtful, so he gently reminded her that she couldn't always put herself in other people's situations without first considering her own.

Her friends were worried about her and told her she needed to spend more time alone. They knew her dedication to helping others in the past and hoped that she would continue along with her own well-being ahead of her relationship with Daniel.

They suggested taking an interest in other things and to be careful with this relationship. Even though they knew how important it was, they told her to take a step back, think about her dreams and goals, and make sure she wasn't giving up her happiness to appease Daniel. Reminding her that a healthy relationship was one in which both partners supported and encouraged each other and where both could follow their own interests while keeping their connection strong.

With love and true care, Bethesda's friends wanted her to find balance in her life, embracing the beautiful qualities that made her the rock of support she was for others while also helping her find happiness.

Although her family and friends were worried, Bethesda stayed true to her beliefs. Her steady drive pushed her forward, and her belief that love is not limited by time or place kept her going. She cared about what other people thought but also knew it was important to follow her heart.

The link with Daniel was a rare and valuable gift that went against what most people would expect. She was sure that their paths had crossed for a reason, that there was a divine plan.
behind the chaos of life. This firm trust in their future gave her the strength to stay on her chosen path, no matter others' opinions.

There were times she had questions and reservations, nevertheless she stayed true to her love for Daniel because knowing their relationship was special and irreplaceable. She wouldn't let what other people thought hurt their relationship or cause her to lose him to someone else. He belongs to her, and only her, and she is ready to take the road ahead of her with unshakable determination because she knows how much they love each other and the strength of their journey together.

Daniel's mother, Mrs. Johnson frustrated that she had to learn about her son's engagement at the beauty shop, set up the scene so she could tell her husband about what she had heard.

"Honey, have you heard about our son?" she asked with worry in his voice. I heard that he is with this girl and wants to get married to her. Do you remember how spontaneous he can be and how often gets in over his head? We've had to come along and help him out of messes before."

Mr. Johnson, engrossed in his newspaper, muttered nonchalantly,

"Mhmm, I heard."

His casual response only added fuel to his wife's frustration.

She felt like he wasn't taking the matter seriously enough, and her voice rose as she continued,

"Did you hear what I said?

This is a serious situation. Daniel needs to forget about marrying that girl and find something else to do!"

Finally lifting his eyes from the newspaper, Mr. Johnson sighed,

"Look, he's a grown man, and he has to make his own choices. We can't keep swooping in to fix everything for him."

Mrs. Johnson, now more irritated, couldn't contain her emotions any longer. She grabbed the newspaper out of her husband's hands and placed it on the table, demanding his full attention.

"This is our son we're talking about! We can't just stand by and watch him make a mistake. We need to talk some sense into him!"

Her frustration resonated with Mr. Johnson, and he knew his wife had a point. Reluctantly, he nodded, realizing that their son's future was at stake as well as the girl he was engaged to, and they needed to act.

"You're right," he finally admitted. "Let's get on the phone and schedule a time for Daniel to come over. We need to talk to him and make sure he's thought this through. And I will also reach out to his best friend Alex and fill him in on what is going on. If anyone could get through Daniel's stubbornness, he will."

With a newfound determination, Mr. Johnson dialed Daniel's

number and arranged for him to visit them that weekend. He was resolute in his belief that they needed to have a heart-to-heart conversation with him about the potential risks and consequences of rushing into marriage.

As they awaited Daniel's arrival, both parents knew that their love and concern for him compelled them to intervene. They hoped that through their guidance and support, their son would gain a clearer perspective and make a decision that would lead to genuine happiness and fulfillment.

On Saturday evening, Daniel arrived at his parents' house, and a few minutes later, the doorbell rang. His dad answered it, and to Daniel's surprise, there stood his friend Alex, the backup plan they had discussed earlier. While unexpected, Daniel didn't think much of it since Alex often visited his parents. As they sat conversating, the topic of his relationship with Bethesda arose. Concerns and questions filled the air as they all wanted to ensure he was making the right decision.

His mother, with a gentle expression, began,

"Daniel, dear, we can't help but worry about this. You've only known this girl for a short time, and marriage is a lifelong commitment. Have you considered if it's the right time?"

Daniel leaned back, trying to appear confident, her name is Bethesda.

"I know it might seem fast, but there's something special about her, Mom. I feel a connection that I've never felt before."

His father chimed in, "We just want to make sure you're not rushing into something you might regret later. Have you thought about your beliefs? Are they aligned with hers?"

Daniel nodded, "We've talked about that, and we have a mutual understanding of each other's values. I believe we can work through any differences."

His best friend, Alex, leaned forward with a concerned expression, "I'm just worried, man. You're taking a big step here. What if she's just after your money or something? You've got to be cautious."

Daniel chuckled, "Come on, Alex, you know me. I can handle myself. I've known her long enough to trust her intentions."

Alex persisted, "Have you told her about the issues you've faced in the past? It's essential to be open and honest about those things."

Daniel's demeanor shifted slightly, but he quickly brushed it off, "I'll tell her when the time is right. I don't want to scare her away or make her doubt our relationship."

His parents and friends exchanged glances, unsure if they could ease their concerns. Daniel's determination to assure them that everything was under control left them hesitant to push further.

Although it wasn't the response she had hoped for, his mom knew she couldn't be demanding. With a mix of love and caution, she spoke gently to him, "Daniel, we just want you to be happy and make the right decision. Take some time to think it through thoroughly."

"I appreciate your concern, but I know what I'm doing," Daniel replied with a hint of defensiveness in his voice. "Bethesda and I have something special, and I won't let anyone, or anything disrupt that."

As the conversation continued, Daniel's assurance didn't waver, even as his loved ones and friend persisted in expressing their concerns. He was resolute in his decision to marry Bethesda, convinced that their love could overcome any challenges.

In the end, they had to respect his choice, hoping that their concerns would prove unfounded. They knew that Daniel was a strong-willed and determined individual, and they could only hope that his confidence in his relationship with Bethesda would lead them to a happy and fulfilling future together.

Daniel believes that he has found a love that filled the hole in his heart and made him complete in ways he had never thought possible. Clearly, he was very close to Bethesda, and he couldn't imagine life without her. Even though his loved ones were worried, Daniel's strong faith in their bond was stronger than their worries. He didn't change his mind about the fact that they had found something truly unique.

He was determined to embrace the love that had formed between them and didn't want other people's opinions to derail it. He was aware that life was full of problems, but he was confident that he and the woman who had won his heart could face them together.

Daniel refused to change his views despite being repeatedly

challenged. He kept his promise to Bethesda and told his family and friends that their relationship was solid and founded on trust and understanding. He never gave up hope that their love could get them through anything.

Bethesda and Daniel stood strong together, never losing faith in their love in the face of adversity. They were aware that their decision was out of the ordinary and contradicted what society and their loved ones expected of them. But they believed that love was something that defied the norms.

To show their loved ones how much they meant to each other, they embarked on an exciting journey. They tried to strengthen their friendship by engaging in mutually meaningful activities and spending quality time together. Bethesda and Daniel both realized that their love would be an inspiration to others.

On the day of Bethesda and Daniel's wedding, the air was full of worry and joy from Bethesda's family and friends who couldn't get over their original doubts and concerns. As much as they wanted Bethesda to be happy, they were worried about how quickly her relationship with Daniel had moved forward.

Both Daniel's and Bethesda's parents, dressed in formal wedding attire, exchanged polite greetings, attempting to hide their true feelings about the situation that was beyond their control. Deep down, all they wanted was for their children to be happy, but the speed at which they had chosen to marry broke their hearts.

Meanwhile, Alex and other friends of Daniel gathered,

silently discussing their concerns among themselves. On the other side, Bethesda's friends, who had been there for her through thick and thin, gathered in the bridal suite. Their faces reflected a mix of smiles and worry as they carefully helped her get dressed, their thoughts quietly contemplating her chosen path.

As everyone took their places, the ceremony begins. Bethesda looked beautiful in her white dress as she walked down the aisle, hoping for an emotional link and acceptance from those she loved. She was happy and excited, but she also felt slightly sad. She wanted their full backing and to know what they wanted. Still, the disapproval stayed, casting a shadow over her joyous day.

Throughout the ceremony, the atmosphere was bittersweet. The guests, while witnessing the beauty of the moment, couldn't help but harbor lingering doubts and concerns. Their whispers carried uncertainty, their eyes occasionally betraying their unease. It was a delicate balance between celebration and apprehension.

CHAPTER 3

UNVEILING SHADOWS

The newlyweds had a fantastic honeymoon in the Caribbean, but even after returning home, they still treated one other with loving glances and smiles of pleasure. Little did they know that their individual expectations and underlying fears would soon surface and put their relationship to the test.

Bethesda and Daniel entered their marriage, each with their dreams and anxieties for the future. Bethesda's heart was overflowing with excitement, and she couldn't believe she'd discovered the guy of her dreams. She imagined a life full of love, laughter, and limitless possibilities. Her thoughts drifted back to the fairy stories she'd read as a youngster, where happy endings were guaranteed.

Unbeknownst to Bethesda, Daniel's thoughts took a different turn. While he was thrilled to be married to her, he couldn't help but recall the dynamics of his parents' relationship, where his mother seemed to hold the reins of control. He was determined that history would not repeat itself in his marriage. Feeling a sense of responsibility, he pondered what changes he needed to make to establish his dominance and maintain a strong presence in their relationship.

Now that the wedding party was just a fond memory, a small change was starting to happen. Once a rock of support and understanding, Daniel started acting like he wanted to control what Bethesda did and how she did it.

At first, it was the subtle remarks about her attire. Daniel would casually suggest what she should wear, expressing his preference for certain outfits while subtly implying that others were less desirable. Bethesda, eager to please her husband and unaware of the underlying implications, complied with his suggestions, believing that he was merely offering guidance.

Within a short while, Daniel's controlling behavior went beyond what she wore. He started to ask about Bethesda's phone calls, listening in on her private conversations and asking about how long and what she talked about. She had to tell Sarah several times that she had to stop talking because of an emergency.

After this happened more than once, Sarah put two and two

together and figured out what was happening. She told her family and friends what was going on. At first, Bethesda thought this meant he was worried about her safety and trying to keep her safe. She thought he was trying to keep their relationship strong, so she respected him and didn't mind what he did thinking he was just trying to keep their relationship strong.

Next, Daniel peeks at Bethesda's social media page. He would observe her conversations and ask her about the feedback she received via text from her social circle. He claimed that, as her husband, he was obligated to keep an eye on his wife's online activity to protect their marriage. Once again, Bethesda was so naive that she bought into his excuses, thinking he was trying to keep the relationship safe from the outside world.

Despite the subtle signs of control, Bethesda remained oblivious to the true nature of Daniel's actions. Blinded by her love for him and her trust in their relationship, she interpreted his behavior as acts of protection and devotion. The idea that her husband, the person she had chosen to spend her life with, could exhibit such controlling tendencies seemed unimaginable to her.

Her friends and family, on the other hand, noticed that Bethesda had changed. They saw how, when she and Daniel were with them, she became shyer and more careful, always waiting for Daniel's approval before speaking.

Concerned whispers circulated because they could see her autonomy being slowly weakened, the indicators of a dangerous situation unfolding before them.

They yearned to approach her, to question her about the changes they had witnessed, but they hesitated, fearful of jeopardizing their relationship with her. They understood that Bethesda's perception of the situation was clouded by her love for Daniel, making it challenging to confront her with the reality of his controlling behavior.

In the meantime, Bethesda remained steadfast in her belief that Daniel's actions were driven by a desire to protect her. She continued to see the best in him, attributing his behavior to love rather than control. She convinced herself that she was fortunate to have a husband who cared so deeply, even if it meant sacrificing some of her own independence.

Unknowingly, the shadows of control loomed over her, casting a veil over her perception of reality. The seeds of doubt had been sown, and only time would reveal the true nature of their consequences. As the days turned into weeks and the weeks into months, the question lingered: Would Bethesda eventually unveil the truth, or would she continue to shield herself with the belief that love should overshadow all else?

CHAPTER 4

SHATTERED ILLUSIONS

Time drifted on, and the undercurrent of control in Bethesda's life continued to grow. On a seemingly ordinary day, she excitedly shared a recent photo of herself with an old school friend on her social media page. Little did she know that this innocent act would serve as a catalyst for an explosive outburst that would shatter her.

As Bethesda scrolled through the comments and expressions of joy from her friends, completely absorbed in the positive feedback, Daniel was monitoring her page and had unexpectedly stumbled upon her post. The sight of the photo ignited a spark of jealousy within him, fueling his insecurity and intensifying his need for control. In a fit of rage, he confronted Bethesda.

His once sparkling blue eyes, filled with warmth and affection, now appeared stormy and clouded with jealousy. The love that once radiated from them seemed to diminish, replaced by a burst of resentment and hurt. The vibrant blue hues now carried a dark intensity, reflecting the turmoil within his heart. The usual softness in his gaze was replaced by a piercing gaze that bore into Bethesda, revealing a tumultuous mix of emotions.

With each passing moment, his eyes displayed a shifting spectrum of conflicting feelings—love, anger, hurt, and insecurity. They flickered with a hint of misery, as if struggling to reconcile the conflicting emotions battling within him. Bethesda could sense the transformation in his eyes, a complete departure from the warmth and tenderness she was accustomed to. It was as if a tempest had swept through the familiar depths of his gaze, leaving behind a turbulent storm.

The room seemed to darken as his anger grew.

He then stormed towards her; his face contorted with fury. Accusations flew from his mouth like venomous arrows, accusing her of seeking attention and betraying their trust. The once-calm atmosphere shattered as his voice roared like thunder, laced with a mix of betrayal, anger, and wounded pride. His emotions unleashed, Daniel's gestures became wild and aggressive, as he struggled to contain the overwhelming surge of anger that consumed him.

Caught off guard by his sudden anger, Bethesda felt a wave of fear wash over her. His once comforting presence had transformed into something volatile and unpredictable. She watched in disbelief as Daniel's face distorted with rage, his voice escalating to a volume that seemed to pierce through the walls of their home. The intensity of his reaction shook Bethesda to her core, leaving her trembling and questioning her own actions.

In that moment, the illusion of protection shattered, replaced by the reality of her situation. The fear that had lurked in the shadows of their relationship suddenly materialized, casting a chilling atmosphere over their home. Bethesda realized that her belief in Daniel's actions being driven by love had blinded her to the depths of his controlling behavior.

Overwhelmed by Daniel's intense anger, Bethesda retreated to the solace of her bedroom, seeking refuge from the emotional tempest that had engulfed her. She lay in bed, her thoughts spiraling in a chaotic dance, replaying the scene over and over in her mind.

As she trembled under the weight of his words, Bethesda began to question herself. How had the simple act of sharing a photo led to such an explosive reaction? Was it truly her fault, as Daniel had claimed? Doubt gnawed at her, slowly eroding her confidence and sowing the seeds of self-blame and confusion.

The weight of the situation bore down upon her, leaving her feeling suffocated and helpless. She couldn't fathom why expressing herself and reconnecting with old friends had invoked such a destructive response. The foundations of trust and understanding they had built seemed to crumble beneath her, leaving behind a barren landscape of uncertainty.

In the silence of her room, a tear welled up in Bethesda's eyes, shimmering like a lone droplet of despair. It clung to her lashes for a moment, teetering on the edge of her eyelid, before succumbing to gravity and gently cascading down her cheeks and dissolved into the fabric of her pillow, it marked the beginning of her pool of despair. It symbolized the depth of her pain and the profound sadness that had overtaken her.

Her tear spoke volumes, capturing the overwhelming emotions swirling within her—a mix of hurt, confusion, and a profound sense of loss. It was a tear of shattered trust and a tear that signified the painful realization that their relationship had been marred by a darkness she had never anticipated.

As the tear fell, it was a painful memory of the deep wounds caused by the crazy turn of events. It was a turning point as Bethesda struggled with Daniel's anger and tried to find peace and understanding in the chaos that had shattered their world.

In the aftermath of Daniel's explosive rage, Bethesda found herself navigating a fragile emotional landscape, where every word and action seemed laden with potential danger. Walking on eggshells became her daily routine, as she tiptoed around conversations and interactions, desperately trying to avoid triggering another angry outburst. The once vibrant and confident woman began to retreat into herself, her spirit dimming under the weight of constant fear and anxiety.

Suppressing her own desires and emotions became her coping mechanism, a sacrifice she made in hopes of pacifying Daniel's mood swings. She swallowed her own needs quietly and buried them deep inside, as if they were heavy loads to carry. The vibrant colors of her personality begin to fade, replaced by a muted palette of obedience and submission.

Inside, Bethesda secretly wanted the harmonious, loving partnership she had always imagined. She clung to the good times they'd shared, hoping against hope that his latest outburst was a rare occurrence in their generally harmonious relationship.

She longed for the warm embraces, funny conversations, and continuous encouragement she had formerly known. Although she tried to put it out of her mind, she couldn't deny the nagging suspicion that this occurrence indicated underlying problems in their relationship.

Haunted by the recent incident, Bethesda decided to keep her family and friends in the dark about what was happening to her. Even though the situation was very bad, she didn't want to bother her friends and family with her marriage problems. She didn't tell them because she feared their worry and possible judgment. She also didn't tell them because she was afraid that telling them about her pain would somehow ruin the picture of the perfect life she had carefully built.

Silently, she will have to carry the weight of her troubles, in her heavy heart of unspoken pain. Fighting with her feelings behind closed doors, desperately looking for comfort and answers in the shadows of loneliness, that made her feel even worse, as she deals with the rough seas of her relationship alone.

Bethesda ached for a sign of hope, a glimmer of light that could lead her out of this darkness. She held on to the idea that things could get better, that love could win over the chaos that had taken over their lives. But as each day went by, the cracks in her willpower got more extensive, and it seemed harder and harder to find a way to heal.

She wanted the love and safety she thought she had found in Daniel, but fear and unease kept eating in her spirit. The rose-colored glasses she used to look at her relationship with her husband broke when she realized his anger had scared her.

As the cracks in their relationship deepened. Would she have the courage to face the dark truth about her husband and hold on to fading dreams of love? The answer was still unclear, and her heart, which used to be full of hope, now felt laden with uncertainty and fear.

CHAPTER 5

REDISCOVERING LOVE AMONG DOUBT

On that particular day, while Bethesda was enjoying her well-deserved day off from work, she received an unexpected call from Daniel. His voice held a hint of excitement as he informed her that he had a surprise in store for her. Intrigued yet cautious, she listened attentively as he described what awaited her.

Soon enough, a delivery man arrived at their doorstep, carrying a bouquet of roses and a beautifully wrapped package. As she opens it there was a common pink dress. Although it was nice, she couldn't help but raise an eyebrow at the choice of color, as Daniel knew all too well that pink was not her preferred hue. Alongside the gifts was a card, extending an invitation to a romantic night out.

Initially, confusion clouded Bethesda's mind like a dense fog. She questioned whether this was a genuine gesture or if there was a hidden motive behind the surprise. Her heart was on the edge of a cliff, teetering between doubt and a little bit of hope. It wanted to believe that Daniel's surprise was real and to find comfort in the idea that maybe he didn't mean to hurt her. Yet, the recent turmoil they had experienced left her cautious, guarded against the possibility of being deceived once more.

As the hours ticked by, anticipation filled the air, intertwining with the uncertainty in Bethesda's heart. She couldn't help but question whether her doubts were founded or if they were merely products of her wounded trust. The conflicting emotions waged an internal battle, leaving her torn between guarding herself against potential disappointment and embracing the glimmer of hope that lingered within.

But as Daniel returned home from work, his eyes filled with anticipation, her doubts began to melt away. There was a genuine sparkle in his gaze, an eager flicker that spoke volumes. In that moment, the love she had once known surged within her, reaching out to touch the corners of her soul.

Her defenses softened, and a sense of relief washed over her. The lines of skepticism that had etched themselves on her face began to fade, replaced by a cautious but growing sense of trust erasing the remnants of doubt that had clung to her thoughts. In that fleeting instant, hope triumphed over uncertainty.

It was as if the stress of their recent problems eased for a moment, and a spark of hope lit their way forward. Bethesda let herself get caught up in the moment and even dared to hope that they could find their way back to the love they once had.

Together, they prepared themselves for what promised to be a memorable evening as she filled with a sense of reluctance, found herself surrendering to Daniel's choice of wearing the unflattering pink dress that clung awkwardly to her figure, concealing the natural beauty and confidence that radiated from within. Though her heart longed to wear the midnight blue gown that accentuated her curves and made her feel like the best version of herself, she suppressed her own desires, fearing the consequences of defiance.

As Daniel took charge, he proceeded to instruct Bethesda on every detail of her appearance, from the jewelry even if it did not resonate with her personal taste. Reluctantly, she adorned herself with accessories that felt foreign and mismatched, struggling to find a connection between her true self and the image that Daniel sought to portray.

Her hair, once a source of pride and individuality, became subject to Daniel's meticulous guidance. He insisted on a particular style that mirrored his vision for the evening, further eroding Bethesda's autonomy over her own appearance. As each strand was carefully arranged according to his instructions, she felt her identity slipping away, replaced by a facade that catered solely to Daniel's desires.

In this moment, Bethesda's spirit dimmed, and her confidence took a backseat to the overwhelming pressure to conform. She yearned to express herself authentically, to embrace her own sense of style and beauty. Yet, the weight of Daniel's expectations hung heavily upon her, stifling her voice and suppressing her individuality.

As she stood before the mirror, dressed in an ill-fitting pink dress and adorned with jewelry that felt foreign on her skin, Bethesda couldn't help but feel a sting of loss. The mirror reflected not just her physical appearance, but the compromise of her self-expression and the erosion of her confidence. A part of her silently mourned the vibrant woman who had once fearlessly embraced her own sense of style and stood tall in her own uniqueness.

In the midst of this internal struggle, Bethesda's gaze met Daniel's in the mirror's reflection. Her eyes pleaded for understanding, for the freedom to be herself once more. Yet, she sensed his unwavering determination to mold her into an image that suited his own desires.

Bethesda tried to hide her sadness by pushing herself to smile. As she got ready to go out into the night, her desire to bring back the love that used to be strong was greater than her dislike of Daniel's control over how she looked. She continued to believe that this night would change the darkness that overshadowed their relationship.

Even though she was still sad, she was willing to put

it aside for a while, hoping that the night events would bring them closer together. She longed for a connection, a real moment of closeness that would remind them both of how much they had loved each other in the past.

Bethesda knew she would have to wait until another day to fight for her uniqueness and identity. For now, she chose to put their relationship first, even if it meant sacrificing her happiness. She watched as Daniel meticulously dressed himself paying attention to every detail. He tried to be charming and sophisticated and didn't want to reveal his hidden secret. His clothes showed that he had great taste and wanted to show himself in the best light.

Daniel wore a well-fitted black suit showing off his muscular body, and the jacket hung confidently over his broad shoulders. The sharp lines of his suit were emphasized by the contrast between the brightness of his white shirt and the darkness of his suit.

He was holding several ties. Each one was carefully chosen to complement his suit. There was a little silence in the room when Bethesda mentioned that a pink tie would go well with her outfit. The stillness was deafening, and Daniel's expression indicated he disliked what was happening.

He respectfully but firmly declined the idea, instead opting for a tie that gave him a polished grace that suited his personality. As he meticulously fastened the tie, it became evident that Daniel's intention for the evening was all about him rather than matching Bethesda's outfit.

His shoes were cleaned to a mirror-like shine, which showed how much he cared about even the most minor details. Every step he took would show his determination to come across as a man of elegant taste.

She was aware of his outright rejection of her proposal, yet she was obligated to follow his advice even though it prevented her from expressing her individuality. It demonstrated his determination to hide his flaws to make a lasting impression.

She saw visions of his expectations as they stood next to each other in the mirror. Bethesda could sense the tense atmosphere. She was aware that everything they participated in together would reflect the strength of their relationship. Still, she couldn't help but be upset that they had squandered an opportunity to bond. The way they prepared for the night out revealed how dissimilar they were. Despite their disparate preferences and styles, she hid her melancholy in the hope that this outing may bring them together.

Daniel urged Bethesda to close her eyes and escorted her gently out the front door with an expression of surprise. As he spoke to her to open her eyes, the excitement grew. A white limousine equipped with a chauffeur awaited their arrival. Bethesda couldn't help but feel a wave of exhilaration mixed with amazement as they entered the gorgeous vehicle.

The limousine whisked them away to their favorite love spot, a place that held countless cherished memories from the early days of their courtship. There, among the familiar ambiance, they danced and embraced just as they had on their very first date.

In those magical moments, Bethesda found herself caught up in the enchantment of the night. The worries and uncertainties that had plagued her mind seemed to dissipate, replaced by the intoxicating bliss of their connection. Every touch, every word whispered in her ear, reinforced her belief that her marriage was unbreakable, that the doubts she had harbored were merely figments of her imagination.

As the night ended, they reluctantly left their sanctuary, stepping back into the comforting embrace of the waiting limousine. The intimacy they had shared lingered, carried forth into the bedroom as the warmth of their bodies pressed together, the softness of their shared breath, served as a reaffirmation of the love they had built. In that intimate moment, all prior doubts and uncertainties seemed to vanish, replaced by a newfound conviction. Awakened the next morning entwined in each other's arms, Bethesda chose to dismiss the nagging suspicions that her mind had conjured, attributing them to illusions or external forces attempting to undermine the sanctity of their bond.

In the afterglow of their night of pleasure, Bethesda felt a renewed sense of hope. She clung to the belief that the surprises and moments of magic they shared were a testament to the strength of their love. Her mind, once clouded by uncertainty, now brimmed with optimism for their future together. With a determined heart, she vowed to cherish these moments and let go of the shadows that had threatened to dim their happiness.

Bethesda and Daniel continued to bask in the afterglow of their enchanting night. The memory of the surprise remained etched in Bethesda's mind, a beacon of reassurance in the face of any lingering doubts. The way Daniel had orchestrated the evening, carefully curating every detail, had convinced her that their love was unshakeable.

Their days were filled with laughter, shared adventures, and quiet moments of intimacy. Bethesda cherished the way Daniel's presence could light up a room, and she reveled in the way he made her feel like the most cherished person in this world. The doubts and uncertainties that had once whispered in the corners of her mind seemed to fade into the background, drowned out by the symphony of their growing connection.

CHAPTER 6

UNFORESEEN EXPECTATIONS

Bethesda never expected that her life would take such an unexpected turn. As she navigated the intricacies of her relationship with Daniel, circumstances led her down a path she had never envisioned. It all began with the news that she was pregnant.

The moment Bethesda discovered she was carrying a child, a whirlwind of emotions swept through her. Confusion, surprise, and a hint of fear coursed through her veins. She had always been cautious about starting a family, cherishing her independence and the financial flexibility that came with it. Her dreams were centered around reaching the peak of her professional success before even considering the idea of having children.

Daniel, on the other hand, reacted with sudden joy at wanting to be a father and shared it with her. His happiness stemmed from a desire to exert control over Bethesda, to always have her within his grasp. He saw the pregnancy as a justifiable reason to insist that Bethesda quit her job for the sake of her health and that of their unborn child.

In order for this to happen he would have to reassure her that he was fully capable of providing for their every need. But Bethesda couldn't shake off the internal conflict that brewed within her. She cherished her career and the sense of accomplishment it brought. The thought of relinquishing her financial independence felt suffocating, as if a part of her identity was being sacrificed.

As the days passed, Bethesda found herself torn between her love for giving Daniel the child he always wanted and the deep-rooted desire to maintain control over her own life. She contemplated the potential impact that motherhood would have on her ambitions and aspirations. Could she strike a balance between her career and being a mother? Was it fair to deny herself the joy of having a child simply because it didn't align with her predetermined timeline? Would she be able to fulfill her aspirations while also being the mother she wanted to be?

Late at night, in the solitude of her thoughts, Bethesda wrestled with her conflicting emotions. She wondered if she could find a compromise, a way to pursue her dreams while embracing the journey of motherhood. Yet, doubt gnawed at her heart. She feared that having a child would require sacrifices she wasn't ready to make.

Finally mustering the nerve to sit down and discuss her concerns with Daniel, she did so. She drew a deep breath and began to speak, her voice cracking with emotion as she described her uncertainty and her determination to maintain employment and her financial independence.

"Daniel, I've been thinking a lot about our situation, and I wanted to talk to you about something that's been weighing on my mind. I appreciate your happiness and support regarding the pregnancy, but I can't help feeling conflicted about quitting my job."

Daniel extended his hand to grip Bethesda's while grinning with happiness.

"Bethesda, my darling, I realize this news may have caught you off guard, but please know that my happiness results from my wish to look after you and our child. I want the best for you both, and that involves giving your health and well-being top priority. A wave of warmth and anxiety swept across her.

Although she appreciated Daniel's compassion, she was also worried about losing her independence and hopes for the future.

"I appreciate your concern, Daniel, but quitting my job feels like a significant sacrifice for me. I've always valued my independence and the financial flexibility it provides. I have dreams and goals that I wanted to achieve before starting a family."

With a reassuring tone in his speech, Daniel squeezed Bethesda's hand.

"My sweetheart, I don't want you to feel like you have to completely abandon your dreams. I think we can strike a good balance between your professional goals and your motherly duties. But right now, we need to focus on you and the baby's health. I am confident in my ability to meet our financial obligations.

Bethesda looked into Daniel's eyes, searching for understanding and common ground.

"I want to believe that we can find a way to make it work, Daniel. But I also worry about losing my financial independence and the sense of accomplishment I get from my career. Can we explore other options? Maybe we can discuss creating a support system that allows me to continue working while still being present for our child."

Daniel knew in order to achieve his desire he needed to give her the persona that she was looking for. Therefore, for now he softened his expression.

"Bethesda, I hear your worries and understand your desire to maintain your independence. Let's explore those options together. We can work on finding a support system that allows you to pursue your career while also being there for our child. I don't want you to feel like you're giving up your dreams entirely. We'll find a way to make it work, I promise. But I do want you to be a full-time mom to until our son or daughter turns two."

A spark of hope ignited in Bethesda's heart. She appreciated Daniel's openness to hear her out and try to see things from her point of view because it had created the possibility of a compromise.

"Thank you, Daniel. And I will honor your wishes to be there for our child until the age of two. It means a lot to me that you're willing to consider other options. Let's take the time to explore different possibilities and create a plan that works for both of us. I believe that together, we can find a way to balance our aspirations and our responsibilities as parents."

Daniel nodded, disguising his genuine feelings by assuring her that he is dedicated to achieving that balance with her, and that they would speak openly and make decisions that prioritize their shared vision for constructing a life that meets both their objectives and the love they have for their child.

In that moment, Bethesda realized that although their paths might be divergent, they had a shared commitment to their relationship, their individual dreams, and the well-being of their growing family. Bethesda knew that an open and honest conversation was crucial for the well-being of their relationship and the future of their family.

VOICES OF WOMEN

Before I met my husband, I lived my life feeling unworthy of love. I was in constant despair trying to prove my character and my pure intentions to better the World. However, I prayed every night to find a partner that would love me through my hardships but also be able to allow me the simple joys in life that exist. I was patient and did not settle until I felt in my soul that this was my person.

Meeting my husband, I felt an instant connection and I could see his heart immediately. He had hardships in his past relationships but as the Proverb 18:22 "He who finds a wife finds what is good and gets favor from the LORD." He has always cherished me, supported my aspirations, and accepted my flaws with forgiveness. "Eve was the answer to Adam's loneliness" (Genesis 2:18)

I am treasured more than rubies and I spend every waking moment to show the same sanctuary and unconditional love to my husband because of his faith, strength, and the way he walks in this life to create and protect all the purities this World deserves.

Monica

CHAPTER 7

SHARING THE NEWS

Bethesda's heart raced with anticipation as she prepared to reveal her pregnancy to her loved ones. A mixture of excitement and anxiety swirled within her, reflecting the conflicting emotions she had been wrestling with.

Daniel, though hesitant at first, had finally agreed to allow her family and friends to visit. He was determined to show his love and support for Bethesda, even though he was still guarded about their reaction. He knew that opening their home to visitors meant relinquishing some of the control he held dear, but he understood how important it was for Bethesda to share this moment with her loved ones.

As her family and friends arrived, both greeted them with warmth and affection, embracing each one with hugs and kisses. The atmosphere was filled with joy and laughter, but underneath it all, she felt the weight of the news she was about to share. In the living room, surrounded by her closest loved ones, Bethesda took a deep breath and mustered the courage to speak.

"Everyone, I have something important to share with you. Daniel and I are expecting a baby", watching as the reactions on their faces changed from curiosity to surprise and delight.

As the news sank in, her loved ones showered her with congratulations and expressions of happiness. There were tears of joy and warm embraces, making Bethesda feel the love and support of those closest to her. She saw her family and friends rallying around her, and it brought a sense of relief and reassurance.

Bethesda's best friend, Sarah, held her hand tightly, excitement radiating from her.

"Oh, my goodness, Bethesda! This is incredible news! I'm so happy for you and Daniel! You're going to be an amazing mother." Bethesda smiled, grateful for Sarah's unwavering support. However, she couldn't help but notice a hint of concern in her friend's eyes.

"Thank you, Sarah. It means a lot to me. But I must admit, I never thought this would happen now. I had always envisioned focusing on my career before starting a family."

Sarah nodded, her expression empathetic.

"I understand, Bethesda. You've always been driven and

determined to reach the pinnacle of success in your career. It's natural to feel a sense of conflict when unexpected blessings come along. But remember, being a mother doesn't mean giving up on your dreams entirely. You can find a way to balance both, just as you've always wanted."

Bethesda's heart swelled with gratitude for Sarah's words of encouragement. She felt a glimmer of hope that maybe her aspirations weren't completely out of reach. As the gathering continued, Bethesda's mother, Martha, approached her cautiously, a mixture of joy and concern etched on her face.

"Bethesda, my dear, congratulations on the news. I'm thrilled to become a grandmother. However, I can't help but remember your strong desire to establish yourself in your career before becoming a mother. Are you sure you're ready for this?"

Bethesda hesitated; her mind filled with doubt. She understood her mother's concerns and shared them to some extent.

"Mom, I appreciate your concern. It's true that I had planned to achieve certain milestones in my career before starting a family. Right now, I do not have a choice. I am pregnant. Daniel and I have been discussing how to make it work. We want to find a way for me to continue with my career even during pregnancy and after the baby is born. It won't be easy, but we believe it's possible. I solely trust him that he will help me."

Martha's face softened but worry still lingered in her eyes. "My dear, I want nothing more than for you to be happy and fulfilled. But remember that being a mother is a tremendous responsibility. It will demand your time and energy, especially in the early years. I hope you and Daniel have thoroughly thought through the practical aspects and challenges that lie ahead."

Bethesda nodded; her voice tinged with uncertainty.

"I understand, Mom. It's a journey filled with unknowns, but we're determined to find a way to make it work. I want to create a life where I can be both a loving mother and a dedicated professional. I know it won't be easy, but I believe in our ability to find a balance."

As the conversation continued, Bethesda felt a mix of emotions within her - hope, doubt, and a determination to prove that she could forge her own path. The doubts expressed by her loved ones echoed within her, causing her to question whether she could truly have it all.

However, admist the celebration, Daniel's parents were absent. Bethesda had hoped to include them in this momentous occasion, but Daniel's strong disagreement had prevailed. She felt a pain of sadness, wishing that she could share this joy with his side of the family as well.

Nonetheless, Bethesda was grateful for the overwhelming love and support she received from her own family and friends. Their presence reminded her that she was not alone on this journey and that she had a strong network of love surrounding her.

In that moment, Bethesda knew that she had made the right decision to share this news with her loved ones. Their genuine happiness and unwavering support gave her the strength to face the challenges ahead, knowing that she was not alone in this new chapter of her life.

But deep down, Bethesda knew that her desire for a fulfilling career and motherhood were not mutually exclusive. She was willing to put in the hard work, make the necessary sacrifices, and find a way.

CHAPTER 8

THE BETRAYAL

Bethesda thought she had found solace in the conversation with Daniel. She believed that they had reached a mutual understanding, a shared commitment to finding a balance between their dreams and their roles as parents. But little did she know that Daniel's seemingly supportive words concealed a deeper betrayal.

Bethesda threw herself into researching and exploring potential solutions that would allow her to continue working while caring for their child. She spent countless hours devising plans, networking, and seeking out support systems that could help her maintain her independence.

Yet, within her efforts, Bethesda noticed a growing

distance between her and Daniel. His once supportive and attentive demeanor had transformed into a detached and aloof presence. Her worries multiplied, and she couldn't help but question his true intentions.

One evening, Bethesda decided to confront Daniel, hoping to shed light on the change she had observed in their relationship.

"Daniel, I've noticed a shift between us lately. It feels as if you've become distant, and it's causing me great concern. What's going on? We promised to work together on finding a balance, but I feel like I'm navigating this journey alone."

Daniel moved uncomfortably in his seat, avoiding Bethesda's gaze.

"Bethesda, I've been doing some thinking, and I've come to the realization that it would be best for you and the baby if you focus solely on being a mother. I understand your desire to continue working, but I believe it's in the best interest of our child for you to be fully present. That is why I submitted your two weeks resignation notice on last week Monday. This upcoming week will be your last week, sweetheart. You need to start preparing your body for the extra weight and rest needed to carry the baby. Also think about how nice it will be not to have to get up early and go out in the hustle and bustle of traffic."

Bethesda's heart sank as his words echoed in her mind. She had trusted him, believed that he respected her ambitions and desires. Yet, his sudden change of heart felt like a betrayal.

"How can you say that Daniel? We discussed finding a balance, supporting each other's dreams. This feels like a complete turnaround from what we had agreed upon. I can't believe you're asking me to give up my career and financial independence completely."

Daniel's voice softened, but his firmness remained unyielding.

"I know it's difficult to accept, Bethesda, but I truly believe it's for the best. I want to provide for you and our child, to ensure that you both have everything you need. By focusing solely on motherhood, you can give our child the attention and care deserved."

Anger and disappointment rose within Bethesda because she had counted on his help, but this action that he made crushed her.

"How can you decide something like that for me? This is my life, my occupation, and my dreams. I thought you were my partner and that you cared about my goals. I can't believe you would do something like this to break my trust. It wasn't your duty to submit my two-week resignation without my permission."

She tried hard not to cry, but Daniel's betrayal hit her like a ton of bricks, and she couldn't stop the tears from falling. All she could think about was how in control he made her feel, even though he pretended to be worried and used this to control her. She starts to dislike what he did, which makes her feel sick to her stomach. The truth about how he felt emerged out of the shadows and shattered the basis of their relationship.

But Bethesda's trust was broken when she discovered the

person, she loved had made choices without her permission.

Daniel was worried that Bethesda would discover his secret because of this choice he made for her. He didn't know this would affect her so strongly that she would question his intentions. He knew he had to do something quickly to get her to stop thinking about him, and he swiftly extended his hand to comfort her, but she rejected it. Daniel keeps trying to explain himself as she moves away from him.

"No, Bethesda, I didn't betray you. I'm just trying to determine what will be best for my family. I was trying to keep you and our child safe. Please don't think that I'm trying to stop you from speaking your mind or getting what you want. I only want the best for the people I care about."

"Daniel, the most important thing in a relationship is trust. You made choices that had a direct effect on my life, but you didn't involve me in the process. You think this will help me, but I don't see it that way. It feels like someone is invading my privacy and trying to run my life. This is crucial to me right now. I can try to forget about it, but who knows if it won't happen again? It needs to be fixed right away. You need to be honest with yourself about what you did and take blame for it. If you don't, you'll always think you've done the right thing, even though you haven't. I can't ignore the feeling that I've been betrayed. I need some time alone to think about what this means for us and for me."

After sharing those words, Bethesda got up, her heart heavy with sadness and a deep sense of loss. As she walked away, she wished he knew what he had done and how she felt about it. Bethesda knew she would have to learn to trust him again, but she needed time to heal from the pain in her heart first.

She curled up in the fetal position on the couch and vowed to keep her freedom, fight for her dreams, and build a future that respected her individual needs. She was determined to move on from the betrayal and make a new path for herself, one that fit her needs and was led by her strong spirit.

CHAPTER 9

BETHESDA'S STRUGGLES

As Bethesda faced the reality of becoming a mother, a newfound fire ignited within her. She refused to let Daniel or societal pressures dictate her choices. Instead, she was determined to carve her own path, embracing the unknown with open arms and the transformation that was coming her way.

Unbeknownst to her, the arrival of this precious life would not only reshape her plans but also unveil a reservoir of strength and determination she hadn't realized she had. Bethesda was on the cusp of an extraordinary chapter, where love, personal development, and the pursuit of her aspirations would converge in ways she could never have foreseen, painting her journey with unexpected and exquisite shades of beauty. A few weeks later, Bethesda's phone rang, and she quickly answered it.

"Hello?"

"Hi Bethesda, it's your boss here. How have you been?"

"Oh, hi! I've been good, thank you. How about you?"

"Great, thank you. So, I wanted to talk to you about your resignation. I saw it in my emails, and I was quite surprised. You're a valuable member of our team, and I wanted to understand your reasons."

Bethesda taking a deep breath "Yes, I did submit my resignation. It's been a struggle to balance work and... my personal life."

"I see. Can you elaborate a bit more? I know you've always been committed to your job."

"Well, the thing is, I'm pregnant. And as much as I love my job, I've been finding it hard to manage everything. I want to be there for my child, but I also don't want to give up on my career."

Her boss was surprised. "Congratulations, Bethesda! I had no idea. Thank you for sharing this with me. I can understand how challenging this must be for you."

"Thank you. It's been quite overwhelming. I want to be the best mother I can be, but I also don't want to lose my professional identity."

"I completely understand your concerns. We value you a lot,

Bethesda, and I'd hate to see you leave. What if I told you we could work something out to help you manage both your career and your new responsibilities?"

Bethesda was intrigued. "What do you mean?"

"How about this: I've seen your dedication and your skills. What if we offer you the opportunity to work remotely? You'd have more flexibility in managing your time and taking care of your family."

She was overcome with joy.

"Remote work? That's an interesting option. I didn't think this was possible."

"We want to support our employees in every way we can. You've been an asset to our team, and I believe we can find a way for you to continue contributing while also being there for your family."

"That sounds amazing, honestly. I miss working with the team, and this might be the perfect solution.

"I'm glad to hear that. Take your time to think it over. Once you are ready send me an email and we'll discuss the details."

"Thank you so much for this opportunity. I really appreciate it."

"Of course, Bethesda. We value you, and we want to make sure you're happy with the choices you make."

'I'll definitely think about it and get back to you soon."

"Sounds good. Take care, and congratulations again!"

When Bethesda hangs up the phone, she feels a rush of happiness. She couldn't wait to tell Daniel the news, which she thought might bring them closer to the peaceful life she wanted, but a slight worry nagged at her. She is curious about how he will respond to this unexpected turn of events since she knows his view of her career may not be the same as hers. She knew in her heart that this was the best way for her to handle being a mother and working simultaneously. But for now, she decided to savor this victory on her own and find the right time to reveal the good news to him.

After giving it some thought, she wrote an email to her boss thanking him for the chance to work from home and officially accepting it. She chose each word carefully to show how excited she was to keep adding to the team and how much she was looking forward to being a mom-to-be. She felt a mix of joy and anticipation as she hit the "Send" button. This was a big step toward her goal of a healthy and satisfying life, and she couldn't wait to see how this choice would affect her journey from here on out.

Overriding the feeling of anticipation, she remained happy, clutching the news from her boss, who had successfully persuaded her to cancel her resignation and work remotely. For a long time, she struggled with figuring out how to be a mother who worked. It had been a difficult pill for her to swallow because she had worked hard to get where she was. At the same time, the thought of losing out on her child's early years and being unable to embrace parenting weighed heavily on her heart.

Bethesda's sense of empowerment surged as she embraced the opportunity to work remotely. Recognizing the potential of this arrangement, she saw a path where she could actively engage in her child's milestones, cherish those priceless first moments, and experience the gratification of parenthood without compromising her career objectives. She was overjoyed at the likelihood of having the best of both worlds—the love of her child and the satisfaction of her career.

After making her decision, Bethesda realized that delaying her revelation to Daniel could yield a delightful surprise. This was her chance to unveil her discovery as a solution to their problem, a secret Ace up her sleeve that could transform their circumstances. She held onto the anticipation, envisioning Daniel's joy and understanding once he learned of her decision.

With a confident smile on Bethesda's lips, she decided to savor the moment a little longer. She wanted to bask in the happiness that was sure to surround their home when she eventually shared the news. She understood that this revelation would mark the beginning of a fresh chapter in their journey - one where they could celebrate parenthood while continuing to chase their individual dreams.

"Yes," Bethesda thought to herself, "he cannot refuse this. I have found the perfect balance, and together, we will create a life that is truly fulfilling in every way."

On her first day of remote working, Bethesda was determined to make the most of it. She carefully planned her work hours to align with Daniel's schedule, ensuring that she would be fully available for her job while also taking care of her responsibilities as an expectant mother.

With her new arrangement, Bethesda would start her work as Daniel left for his job in the morning. The early hours allowed her to focus and dive into her tasks without any distractions. She relished the peace and quiet, knowing that she could dedicate her full attention to her professional responsibilities.

Throughout the day, Bethesda maintained a diligent work ethic, ensuring that she met deadlines and delivered high-quality work. She was determined to showcase her capabilities as a working mom, proving to both her and Daniel that she could successfully balance both roles.

As the clock ticked closer to Daniel's usual departure time from work, Bethesda wrapped up her work tasks, always making sure to finish thirty minutes before his scheduled return. This gave her enough time to transition from her professional responsibilities to preparing for his arrival, creating a seamless shift from her remote work to her duties as a wife and soon-to-be mother.

Deep within her heart, Bethesda held onto a quiet hope. It wasn't about tricking or manipulating Daniel, but about showcasing her capability to thrive in her career while fully embracing motherhood's joys. As he saw her dedication and the positive outcomes of her remote work, she believed Daniel would understand her choice and find harmony in the balance she strived for.

Bethesda often immersed herself in daydreams while she went about her everyday activities, picturing Daniel's ecstatic reaction.

These dreams reenacted the moment she would eventually reveal her successful strategy for working remotely, bringing positive change into their lives.

She saw herself sitting across from Daniel, relaxed and satisfied. She begins to describe her story, including how her supervisor recognized her value and persuaded her to reconsider her resignation and accept remote work. This change promised a smooth integration of her work and personal life.

Her daydreams ignited with her sharing her achievements, outlining the concrete fruits of her labor. She could practically hear Daniel's amazement and adoration as she described the finished projects, the accolades from her coworkers, and her growing status within the company.

Bethesda imagined his laughter and the pride in his eyes as he gave her words of encouragement and support, recognizing her professional accomplishments and his wholehearted acceptance of her decision for remote work as evidence of her passion for supporting their family and her career.

Daniel's doubts vanished in these dreams, replaced by new clarity. They would come together, celebrating this newfound equilibrium—where she excelled as both a mother and career woman. Reality returned as Bethesda left her daydreams. Nonetheless, these visions gave her optimism that they would soon come true. She was confident that her dedication and perseverance would bear fruit, allowing her to show Daniel the tangible benefits of her decision. Her dream remained - a future where their baby's arrival was celebrated, knowing they had harmoniously united their professional and family lives.

The pressure of working long hours in front of the computer while pregnant affected her body and mind as the weeks passed.

She was becoming increasingly fatigued, making maintaining her usual energy and enthusiasm difficult. She became exhausted and stressed out because she wasn't getting enough sleep.

Daniel, always on the lookout, noticed that Bethesda's behavior had changed. He was worried when he saw how tired she was and how often she went to bed much earlier than usual. His mind was full of questions, and he couldn't help but ask her repeatedly if everything was okay.

With a gentle smile masking her hidden secret, Bethesda replied to Daniel's concerns, attributing her exhaustion to the natural progression of her pregnancy. She assured him that it was a combination of the physical demands of carrying their child and the adjustments her body was undergoing.

Bethesda struggled each passing night, for the freedom to rest without the added burden of secrecy. She fought to keep up the front that her pregnancy was the only reason she was tired. She wanted to tell Daniel the truth about why she went to bed so early and how working from home was starting to affect her. She didn't say anything, though, because she knew she wanted to tell him about her success when the time was right.

Yet, as the days went by and her fatigue persisted, Bethesda couldn't help but feel the weight of her secret growing heavier. She knew that the time would soon come to share her accomplishment with Daniel, but the physical and mental strain of keeping it hidden was beginning to test her decision.

VOICES OF WOMEN

In the first place, I give all praise and respect to God. I also want to thank Mrs. Bernice Brown very much for giving me the chance to share a small part of my story with all of you. In many ways, Bethesda, from the book, is like me and my journey. The Bible says in Proverbs 18:22, "He who finds a wife finds a good thing," which shows how important this union is.

Still, we need to be ready mentally, physically, and most importantly, spiritually to be truly ready for this gift. Just like we tell our human father what we want, and he gives it to us when he thinks it's right or when we've earned it, so does our Heavenly Father. He knows when the time is right and gets us ready as brides for the one, He picks to be our life partners.

Like Bethesda, I had to go through heartbreaks to come to this conclusion, and each one made me want to seek the Lord's help even more. During these hard times, God led me to the Book of Esther, where I learned important lessons and learned the essence of womanhood, which I wanted to be.

God prepares our hearts and minds, just like He does
for the men who will become our husbands. As women of
God, we can use the wise words of Proverbs 31:10–31 as a
guide. I think about this Bible verse a lot because I want to
have the traits of a good woman. It has kept me steady as I've
worked to become the woman God wants me to be.

My heart yearns to be not just a loving wife but, more
importantly, to be seen as divine in the eyes of the Lord. To
all the sisters out there, embrace your divine journey with
Him. Amen.

Sherri

CHAPTER 10

SURPRISE!

As Daniel's day wore on, he couldn't shake off a feeling of concern for Bethesda. He had noticed her exhaustion and wanted to do something special to show his support and care. Determined to bring a smile to her face, he made the spontaneous decision to leave work early, hoping to surprise her with a warm and loving gesture.

With anticipation in his heart, Daniel arrived home earlier than usual, eager to greet Bethesda with open arms. However, as he stepped into the house, his excitement transformed into confusion and worry. The once tidy and organized living space was in disarray, and a faint aura of neglect lingering in the air.

Daniel cautiously ventured further into the house, his

footsteps echoing in the silence. He went into the kitchen, but she was not there. As he reached the top of the stairs, he heard the familiar sound of tapping keyboards and the occasional sigh of frustration. It was then that he realized Bethesda was engulfed in something, completely oblivious to his presence.

When he opened the office door, it startled her as she glanced up at him standing in the doorway, with a curious look on his face. Bethesda's eyes widened with a feeling of surprise and guilt as she realized the state of the house and that Daniel had come home early. She had been so engrossed in her work that she hadn't noticed his arrival until that very moment.

Regret washed over Bethesda like a crashing wave as she hurriedly closed her laptop, her focus now solely on Daniel. With a sense of urgency, she rushed towards him, her heart aching with the weight of her apologies. She reached out, gently touching his arm, her voice trembling as she directed her words to him alone.

"Daniel, I am so sorry," Bethesda began, her voice filled with genuine remorse. "I made a decision to work remotely without telling you. I wanted to find a way to embrace both motherhood and my career, to show you that I could excel in both realms. In my pursuit of balance, I kept this plan hidden but I was going to tell you when the time was right. If you allow me, I will share with you what happened."

Her eyes filled with concern, Bethesda continued, her voice cracking with vulnerability. "I understand if you're angry and disappointed. I betrayed your trust, and for that, I am deeply sorry. It was never my intention to deceive you, but in my misguided attempt to prove myself, I lost sight of the importance of open communication and shared decision-making."

She paused, searching Daniel's eyes for any sign of understanding or forgiveness. "I want you to know that I am committed to making things right. I recognize the gravity of my mistake, and I promise to prioritize honesty and transparency from this moment forward. Our relationship deserves nothing less."

Bethesda's hands trembled as she reached out to Daniel, her touch gentle yet pleading.

"Please, Daniel, believe in my love for you and our shared dreams. I will work tirelessly to regain your trust, to show you that my intentions were rooted in a desire to create a beautiful future for our family. Let us find a way to heal and move forward together, hand in hand."

Daniel listened to Bethesda's heartfelt plea, his anger slowly softening as he witnessed the raw emotion in her eyes and the sincerity in her voice. Though still upset, he recognized the depth of her regret and the strength it took for her to admit her mistakes.

In that moment, a spark of understanding ignited within Daniel's heart. He saw the love and dedication that Bethesda had poured into her efforts, albeit in a misguided manner. And as he looked at her, his eyes filled with a mix of pain and hope, he whispered, "Bethesda, we have a long road ahead of us. But I believe in our love, and I know you are willing to work towards healing and rebuilding the mistrust that you've allowed to enter our relationship.

He reached for her hand and drew her close, enveloping her in a tender embrace. From the outside, it seemed as if Daniel had found solace in their physical connection, but within him, a storm of conflicting emotions raged. The pain he felt was not merely a result of Bethesda's actions; it ran deeper, touching the very core of his being.

As his arms encircled her, Daniel battled with an internal turmoil that seemed insurmountable. The weight of betrayal, disappointment, and hurt threatened to consume him. He struggled to reconcile the image he had held of Bethesda - the woman he loved and trusted - with the person standing before him, who had kept such a significant secret.

In that moment, Daniel's embrace held both warmth and pain. He cherished Bethesda, their shared memories, and the dreams they had built together. But alongside those feelings, a sense of loss and shattered trust loomed heavily.

His mind swirled with questions. How could he trust her again? Would their relationship ever be the same? Was forgiveness even possible? The answers eluded him, buried beneath the layers of confusion and anguish that clouded his thoughts.

Daniel's grip on Bethesda grew slightly tighter as he held her, showing the struggle going on inside him. The struggle between his love for her and the immense pain she had caused battled fiercely in his heart. Silent tears escaped from Daniel's eyes, unnoticed by

Bethesda in the depths of their embrace. The pain he felt was not solely directed at her; it reflected his own vulnerability and the profound disappointment that comes with shattered expectations. In that moment, Daniel wrestled with his own emotions, recognizing that the path to forgiveness and healing would be filled with challenges. He yearned for the pain to dissipate, and for the wounds to mend.

As they stood there with their arms around each other, Bethesda could tell that Daniel was feeling a lot of different things. She knew that her apologies and promises wouldn't be enough to make things right between them. It would take kindness, understanding, and a deep knowledge of the pain she had caused him. Bethesda couldn't get rid of the worry that was growing inside her. She knew it would be hard and take a long time to win Daniel's trust back, but that wasn't the only thing that worried her. Would he ever be able to agree with her that she should keep working from home? Would it be a constant reminder to him of how she had hurt him?

Bethesda's heart ached with a mix of hope and worry as the weight of doubt descended over her. She yearned for Daniel to recognize honesty in her motives and comprehend that her pursuit of a rewarding job while being a mother was not intended to harm their relationship but rather to build a life of balance and happiness.

While they were still hugging, Bethesda gathered the confidence to express her worries, her voice trembling with fear. "Daniel, I recognize the suffering I've brought you, and I'll do whatever it takes to make it right. But I also hope you can understand that I want to keep working remotely because I want to create a future where both of our ambitions can come true. Finding a means to be there for our child while pursuing my career goals is the goal - not evading responsibility or neglecting our family.

She held her breath, fearing Daniel's response. Would he reject her plea and insist on a different path? Or would he be open to understanding her perspective and finding a compromise that would honor both their needs?

Daniel's grip loosened, and he looked deeply into Bethesda's eyes. His voice, caring yet laced with uncertainty. "Bethesda, I can't deny that this has shaken the foundation of our relationship. But I also see your passion and determination. I can't promise what the future holds, but I am willing to listen, to understand your perspective, and to explore a way forward that respect both our dreams."

Bethesda's heart flashed with optimism as she listened to Daniel's words echo over and over in her ears.

Chapter 11

A NEW HORIZON

Now Daniel had to deal with the fact that Bethesda wanted
to keep working from home. He couldn't argue with the truthfulness
of what she said or the passion that drove her goals. With each
passing day, his heart eased, and he looked past the pain and
betrayal to see how much they loved each other and how much they
could grow.

When it was quiet and the beautiful sunlight from the setting
sun reflected on their house, Daniel went to Bethesda with a
different perspective. His voice filled the room with restraint and
assurance.

"Bethesda, I've had time to think about everything, and

I've realized that you're wanting to work from home doesn't say anything bad about our relationship. It represents your hopes, dreams, and needs to be fulfilled. I want you to know that you have my backing."

Bethesda reached over and hugged and passionately kissed him. She couldn't help feeling thankful and relieved. The weight on her heart slowly lifted, replaced by a sense of peace and a spark of hope for their future.

She smiled as she reached out to hold Daniel's hand, and their fingers intertwined to signify getting back together.

"Daniel, I can't tell you how much your support means to me," she said with sincere gratitude. "I feel at peace knowing that you understand and care about my dreams. We can make a beautiful life for our growing family if we work together."

In the weeks that followed, their home went through a big change. The once-tense environment calmed down, and Bethesda and Daniel were surrounded by a newfound peace. Their journey to healing had come to a crucial turning point, and they both opened themselves up to the opportunities ahead.

As Bethesda's due date got closer, they were getting more and more excited. Every day, they were getting closer to the birth of their child, and their shared joy made them even closer. Daniel used to have a lot of questions and fears, but he became Bethesda's strength.

He gave everything he had to help her in every way he could. Daniel's love and commitment shone brightly as they went to doctor's appointments together, made sure she was comfortable in the last stages of her pregnancy, and carefully set up the nursery. He became her rock, giving her comfort and company as she went through the roller coaster of feelings that come with getting ready to have a baby.

No longer were late nights filled with tension and silence. Instead, they were filled with talks about everything from the practical parts of being a parent to their hopes for their child's future. They laughed together, enjoying the sweet times and finding comfort in being with each other. Daniel's constant support gave Bethesda the peace of mind she needed, so she could fully enjoy the joy of becoming a mother.

Daniel found a new depth of love and kindness in himself through their journey together. He knew that his presence was important and that it was good for Bethesda's health. Every nice thing he did or word of support he said showed how much he cared about their relationship and the family they were about to start.

Bethesda was amazed by how much their shared experiences had changed them. All the problems they had faced and mistakes they had made seemed to fade away. In their place, a steady connection grew, based on confidence, understanding, and a strong bond that couldn't be broken.

Together, Bethesda and Daniel approached the beginning of her third trimester with a sense of wonder and awe. They cared for and set up the nursery with love, making it a safe place for their child. When it was quiet, they sat beside each other with their hands on

Bethesda's growing belly. They talked about the life they wanted to build as a family.

Their hearts were filled with excitement, but their home was filled with peace. Bethesda was so thankful for how their relationship had changed. With Daniel by her side, she felt better knowing they were a team, ready to face the difficulties of being parents.

The day had come for Bethesda and Daniel to find out the gender. As they sat together in the room, with their hands tightly clasped, the air was full of excitement. The sonographer's words filled the room, and with them came a significant discovery.

The sonographer said, "It's a boy," with a smile. When they heard they would have a son, they were overjoyed and fell in love with the life they were building together.

They began chatting about naming their gorgeous baby boy as they left the doctor's office with a fresh feeling of purpose. They realized that the name they gave him would become a part of who he was and reflect their intentions for him.

Bethesda and Daniel sat in their comfortable living room for hours, conversing and reading baby name books. They ran their fingertips over the pages of names rich in history, meaning, and emotion. Each name had a unique meaning, a story that had yet to be told.

Their voices blended into a beautiful song of love and excitement as they talked about their hopes for their son. Bethesda told her husband that she wanted his name to mean power, resilience, and kindness. Daniel nodded and agreed.

Time seems to stand still as they spent hours on end thinking about the perfect name for him. Weighing the options against their hopes for their son's future, then, in a moment of clarity, a name that touched her heart deeply came to mind.

"Gabriel," Bethesda whispered with a sense of awe in her voice.

When Daniel looked at her, he slowly started to smile.
"Gabriel," he said repeatedly, enjoying how the name felt on his lips. A name that shows bravery, grace, and the spirit of a guardian."

At that moment, they made up their minds. Gabriel was the name they would give to their child.

Motivated by a common goal, Bethesda and Daniel started to imagine a future for Gabriel where he would grow and thrive, surrounded by love, support, and steady direction. They imagined him taking his first steps, saying his first words, and starting on his path.

When they talk about Gabriel, they get closer to each other and rebuild the relationship that had been broken. It was a great time to talk, look at each other lovingly, and hug. Most importantly, they had decided that the first gift they would give their son would be the name Gabriel.

After deciding on a name, Bethesda gently held her growing belly and could feel life moving inside. She whispered, "Gabriel, we can't wait for the day we can hold you in our arms, shower you with love, and watch you grow into the amazing person you are meant to be."

She felt a deep sense of thankfulness. At that time, Bethesda, Daniel, and their soon-to-be-born son Gabriel were all connected by an invisible thread of love that would never break. An indescribable wind of peace that blew away the hard times they had been through making it a faraway memory, replaced by their love, support, and commitment to each other.

Each day brought more excitement but was met with a deep sense of thankfulness and readiness. Bethesda knew she and Daniel had found their way back to each other and were stronger and more capable than ever. She believes that the love and peace in their home would be a good start for the beautiful journey of parenthood ahead.

With Daniel's continuous encouragement and shared purpose, they are ready for the joys, challenges, and many gifts that await them in this next part of their lives.

CHAPTER 12

SHOWERED WITH LOVE

The news of Bethesda's pregnancy had spread throughout their circle of friends and family, filling their hearts with joy and excitement. As the due date drew near, whispers of anticipation filled the air, and Bethesda's loved ones began planning a baby shower to celebrate the imminent arrival of Gabriel.

Bethesda's best friend, Sarah, took the lead in organizing the shower, enlisting the help of their close-knit group of friends and family members. Together, they began on a mission to create a memorable and heartfelt celebration. Sarah's living room became the hub of creativity and collaboration.

They gathered around a table adorned with colorful

decorations, streamers, and tiny baby clothes, their laughter filling the room as they shared stories and exchanged ideas. It was a labor of love, fueled by the shared desire to make Bethesda's baby shower a truly special occasion.

With each passing day, the plans grew more elaborate. They carefully selected a theme that reflected Bethesda's love for nature and adventure. The room would be transformed into a whimsical woodland wonderland, complete with cascading greenery, twinkling lights, and delicate floral arrangements. Every detail was meticulously considered, from the selection of games and activities to the menu that would delight everyone's taste buds. After planning and making changes for weeks, everything was finally just the way they wanted it.

Bethesda's heart was filled with joy, and thankfulness as the long-awaited baby shower neared. She knew that every element reflected the love and care her friends and family placed into preparing the event. But, unbeknownst to her, a cloud of uncertainty hung over Daniel's mind, clouding his judgment and influencing his behavior.

In the final moments leading up to the baby shower, Daniel's concern for Bethesda's well-being took a different turn, influenced by his own insecurities and past experiences. He couldn't shake the memory of the disapproval they had faced from Bethesda's friends and family when they had announced their decision to get married. In his mind, he believed that spending time with them was an opportunity for them to poison her perception of him, increase her doubts and cause dissatisfaction in their relationship.

Because of these beliefs, Daniel made a choice at the last minute that caught Bethesda off guard. He told her she couldn't go to the baby shower because he was worried about her and the baby getting sick at a big party. He told her she had to make a phone call and tell them she ate something that did not agree with her, making her stomach upset and was not able to come.

Bethesda was torn. She cherished her friendships and valued the support of her loved ones, but she also cared deeply for Daniel and feared his reaction if she didn't comply with his wishes. The weight of the situation bore down on her, leaving her uncertain and conflicted. Her mind became a battleground of emotions. On one hand, she felt guilty about lying to her friends, betraying their trust by pretending to be unwell. She appreciated the thoughtfulness they had poured into planning the baby shower, and the idea of disappointing them filled her with sorrow.

On the other hand, Bethesda's love for Daniel and her desire to maintain harmony within their relationship tugged at her heart. She wanted to ease his worries and fears, even if it meant sacrificing her own happiness in the process. The fear of his potential reaction materialized over her, confusing her judgment and making her question her own action in the decision.

Hours before the baby shower, Bethesda stood at the crossroads of her conflicting emotions. She envisions the decorations, the laughter, and the joyous atmosphere, marveling at the thoughtfulness of her friends and family. Yet, a heavy sadness settled within her as she struggled with the weight of the lie she was about to tell.

In her heart, Bethesda yearned for transparency, honesty, and open communication. She longed for a relationship where she didn't have to hide her true feelings or compromise her connection with loved ones. But at this moment, she felt trapped, unsure of how to navigate the delicate balance between loyalty to those she loved and her desire to keep peace with Daniel.

As the minutes ticked by, she found herself standing in front of her phone, her finger hesitating over the dial pad. She knew that whatever decision she made would have consequences, shaping the course of her relationships and her own emotional well-being.

In the depths of her turmoil, Bethesda summoned the strength to pause and reflect. She realized that honesty, vulnerability, and trust were the foundations on which true connections were built. She understood that continuing to hide her true feelings and participating in this web of deception would only deepen the divide between her and her loved ones.

Bethesda made a courageous choice and put the phone down, realizing that she couldn't go through with the lie and resolved to have an open conversation with Daniel, to express her concerns, and to seek a resolution that honored both their relationship and her friendship.

Full of worry and compassion she took a deep breath and gathered her thoughts before starting the talk.

"Daniel, I want to talk to you about the baby shower," she said softly but firmly. "I've been thinking about everything and realized that I can't pretend to be sick." It's unfair to my friends and family and contradicts my values of honesty and authenticity."

Daniel listened intently; his brow furrowed slightly as he pondered what she said. He paused before responding, his voice full of honesty and vulnerability.

"Bethesda, I understand and respect your desire to be truthful. But I'd also like to share my point of view with you. I believe your family and friends will interfere in our relationship, casting doubts in your mind and causing a schism between us."

Bethesda was amazed at his confession. She had sensed his unease before but seeing him express it freely struck a chord with her. She paused to collect her thoughts, ensuring her response was thoughtful and considerate.

"Daniel, I hear your concerns, and I understand why you feel this way," she said calmly but sympathetically. "However, I believe our friends and family have good intentions." They are concerned about us and want what is best for us. They've been a part of our lives for a long time, and their encouragement means a lot to me."

Daniel groaned, with a look of frustration on his face.

"I know they mean well, but it sometimes feels like their opinions and actions get in the way of us." I'm concerned that the more time we spend with them, the more difficult it will be for us to focus on strengthening our family bonds."

Softly she laid her hand on Daniel, " I want you to know how much I value our relationship. Our bond is the core of our family. But maintaining our friendships and connections with loved ones may enhance and assist us in various ways."

Slowly the thoughts that Daniel had begun to disintegrate.

"I see what you're saying. And I don't want to get in the way of you and your loved ones. I just hope we can find a way to prioritize our relationship while still retaining those ties."

Bethesda nodded," I believe we may achieve that balance by communication and setting boundaries. It's critical for us to spend time together as a family while also cultivating meaningful relationships with people who have been a part of our lives."

They sat quietly for a moment, the weight of their conversation lingering. Their mutual understanding and respect left them with hope for finding common ground.

As she allow Daniel's comments to set in, Bethesda was shock to hear that this is the way he felt. She had anticipated a little opposition about attending the baby shower, but his attitude blinded her.

"Sweetheart I appreciate your honesty and willingness to try to see things from a different perspective," "It means a lot to me that you're willing to try something new."

Daniel nodded, "Now I recognized that perhaps I was too

quick to allowed my fears to cloud my judgment." I want to help you, and that requires trying to understand how important your family and friends are in your life."

Bethesda smiled, a sigh of relief overcoming her.

"Thank you so much, sweetheart. Your willingness to push yourself beyond your comfort zone means a lot to me."

Daniel reached out and softly stroked Bethesda's cheek.

Bethesda's heart overflowed with a fresh feeling of optimism and affection for Daniel. "It is not a matter of choosing between you and them but of finding a way for all of us to coexist together."

He smiled. "Exactly. We're a team, and we can overcome any obstacles that come our way."

"Daniel, in light of your openness and our shared commitment to growth, would you like to join me at the baby shower?" Bethesda asked, with excitement in her voice.

"Certainly, Bethesda, I'd be delighted to accompany you! Let us celebrate this wonderful occasion and show our loved ones we are one."

With a burst of enthusiasm, Bethesda rose from her seat. She felt tremendous gratitude as they prepared for the baby shower.

CHAPTER 13

GABRIEL'S ARRIVAL

Bethesda allowed her thoughts to roam through beloved memories of the day. Reaffirming the ties that bound her to her loved ones, the laughing, the sincere chats, and the moments of connection resounded in her mind. She was incredibly grateful that they were in her life. A calmness descended about her as she felt a warm hug of happiness and appreciation for her friends and family. The baby shower symbolized the love and support she needed.

She couldn't help but think of Daniel, and her lips softened into a smile feeling hopeful after seeing him having a good time. Barriers of mistrust between him and her family and friends were coming down. He had been sincere in his dealings with them during the baby shower, and Bethesda had noticed his remarkable openness.

Bethesda clung to the hope that this was a turning moment in their relationship. She could see a brighter future as the shadows of mistrust and doubt that had followed them began to fade.

With her head in her dreams and her heart full of thankfulness, Bethesda gave herself to the soothing rhythm of her breathing nesttled under the cover and went into a deep sleep.

Suddenly she was awoken. Her heart raced with fear and joy as she felt warm all around her. She knew her water had broken . As the truth of the situation hit her, she felt a wave of pain that got worse with each passing second. Bethesda settled herself and turned over to wake Daniel, who was still sleeping.

She said with a sense of urgency, "Daniel, wake up! My water broke, and I am having contractions."

Daniel's eyes shot open as he went from sleep to awake and terrified instantly. He took her suitcase and assisted her in getting to her car. Bethesda's pain in her body grew stronger by the minute, making it harder for her to move. As they rushed to the hospital, she grabbed Daniel's hand tightly, drawing strength from his presence while feeling both excited and frightened.

When Bethesda got to the hospital, the medical staff took over. They led her to a birth room and gave her the needed support and care. As labor pain worsened, Daniel stayed by her side and spoke words of comfort and support. Bethesda found comfort in Daniel's steady presence, gentle touch, and loving words.

Every hour of the painful contractions seemed to last forever. In the short time between, she managed to give Daniel a reassuring smile when she saw how scared he was. As time went on, she started to feel tired, but she knew she couldn't stop until she heard their baby's long-awaited cry. And then, just as the pain was at its worst, with one last push, their loved baby boy took his first breath. His cries filled the room like a melody of life.

At that moment, the pain and tiredness of labor faded into the background, and a huge rush of love took its place. Bethesda believed that the tiny life they had brought into the world, overshadowed every problem and worry casting them far away.

Daniel watched as Bethesda wrapped their son Gabriel in a warm hug. He was happy to see how lovingly and carefully his wife took on her new role as a mother. But underneath that joy was a quiet sense of unease, an itch of fear that he tried hard to hide. He couldn't help but wonder what his role was in her life.

He worried that their new baby might make them forget how close they used to be. He also was concerned about their relationship changing as they progressed through parenthood. He could see the calmness as she held him in her arms, even though she didn't know what he was thinking.

Rejecting this feeling of insecurity, Daniel learned that love can be shared and increased when he saw Bethesda and Gabriel become close. He realized that his worries about being replaced were not true and that their growing family didn't change how much they loved each other as a pair.

Instead, it gave them a chance to grow closer to each other and create memories. In that sweet moment, Daniel decided to accept Bethesda and Gabriel's deep love for each other. He let go of his worries and let himself be taken in by the beauty of their growing family. He understood that their journey wasn't about competition or being replaced. Instead, it was about appreciating the gift that life had given them.

CHAPTER 14

JOURNEY TO UNCOVER SECRETS

Bethesda's desire to visit Daniel's parents had been growing stronger with each passing day. She longed to connect with them on a deeper level and to understand the roots from which Daniel had sprung. She believed that visiting them would not only strengthen their bond as a couple but also provide a sense of completeness to their growing family.

One evening, as they talked in the comfort of their home, Bethesda presented the subject.

"Daniel, I've been thinking. I would really love to visit your parents. It's important to me to know them better and for them to know our baby."

Daniel's eyes blinked with a hint of hesitation, and a veil of unease seemed to settle over his face. He shifted uncomfortably in his seat, his voice laced with apprehension.

"Bethesda, it's not that simple. It's difficult for me to take time off from work, and besides, I'm not sure if it's the right time."

Perplexed by his response, Bethesda pressed on, her voice filled with genuine curiosity. "But why, Daniel? They are your parents, and I want to be a part of their lives. I feel like there's a missing piece in our family puzzle, and visiting them could help bridge that gap."

A brief trace of pain crossed Daniel's eyes, a shadow of unresolved issues.

"It's complicated, Bethesda. You see, my father distanced himself from me when I was young. We never had a strong relationship and when I tried to reachout to him years ago we couldn't see eye to eye, and things haven't been the same since. I've even stopped talking to my mother about him. It's as if he's become a distant memory. In my mind, he is dead."

Bethesda's knew she had to let him see how much she was concern about the situation. She reached out and gently held Daniel's hand, her touch offering reassurance and support.

"Daniel, I understand that there may be unresolved issues between you and your father, but that shouldn't prevent us from making a relationship with your mother. We can navigate this together, as a team."

She could sense the tension building within Daniel as she

pressed him for an answer. His brows furrowed, his jaw clenched, and a impression of frustration rushed in his eyes. She had touched a raw nerve, and it was clear that he was not ready to confront the issue.

"Danny, please," Bethesda pleaded gently, reaching out to touch his arm. "I just want to understand. It's important to me to be a part of your family, to connect with your mother. We can face whatever challenges come our way together."

But Daniel's reaction was not what she had expected. His face hardened, his voice tinged with anger.

"Enough, Bethesda!" he snapped, pulling his arm away. "I've told you it's not the right time, and I don't appreciate you questioning my decision."

Stunned by his sudden outburst, Bethesda recoiled slightly, hurt evident in her eyes. She hadn't meant to push him, but her desire to build bridges and create a sense of unity had clouded her judgment. She watched as Daniel turned away, walking towards another room, leaving her standing there, feeling confused and sad.

Bethesda, tried to steady her emotions and grasped that he was dealing with his own inner struggles, and her persistence had inadvertently pushed him further away. As much as she longed for answers and connection, she realized that respect for his boundaries was crucial.

With a heavy heart, Bethesda slowly followed Daniel into the other room. She found him standing near a window, his back turned to her. She approached him cautiously, her voice soft and filled with sincerity.

"Sweetheart, I'm sorry. I didn't mean to upset you," she said, her words laced with genuine remorse. "I respect your decision, and I understand that you have your reasons. Please know that I only want what's best for us, and I'm here to support you, no matter what."

Daniel remained silent for a moment, his posture tense. Then, he turned toward her, "Bethesda, it's not that I don't want you to be a part of my family. It's just... it's complicated. There are wounds that haven't fully healed, and I need more time to process everything."

She concurred, her gaze meeting his, filled with empathy.

"I understand, Daniel. Healing takes time, and I'll be patient. Just know that I'm here for you, ready to face the challenges and support you through it all."

Inside Daniel felt a little bit of gratitude mingled with a trace of sadness. He reached out and took Bethesda's hand with a his gentle grip.

"Thank you for understanding, Baby. I know it's not easy, but please trust me. I want to protect you and our relationship. I just need some space to figure things out."

Bethesda squeezed his hand, a silent reassurance passing between them. She knew that respecting his boundaries meant giving him the time and space he needed.

As they stood there, hand in hand, Bethesda felt a renewed sense of determination. She would continue to be there for Daniel, supporting him on his own path of healing, even if it meant moving through uncertain territory. Together, they would find their way, one step at a time, towards their future.

Nine months have passed relatively quickly. Bethesda was astonished by how drastically Gabriel was growing. His cheerful babbling and eagerness to crawl amazed them every day. Every action he took was a treasured memory.

Despite her happiness, she couldn't shake the thought that Daniel's parents should be around to enjoy these beautiful moments with her. Bethesda wanted them to witness Gabriel's contagious laughter and cheery smiles. She believed that a strong bond between grandparents and grandchildren was crucial.

Every time she gently brought up the topic, Daniel seemed to deflect or brush it off with vague excuses. She couldn't help but feel a slight bit of disappointment, wondering if he truly understood the significance of this connection. It made her question whether he was as committed as she was to upholding their agreement of including both sides of the family in their lives.

One evening, as Gabriel sat on the living room floor, babbling happily, Bethesda mustered the courage to address her concerns with Daniel. She chose her words carefully, wanting to convey her emotions without sounding accusatory.

"Danny, I can't help but feel a bit disheartened that your parents haven't met Gabriel yet," she began, her voice filled with a mixture of helplessness and longing. "He's growing so quickly, and I want them to be a part of his life, to share in the joy and love that he brings. It's important to me that our families connect and create lasting memories."

Daniel's expression softened, as he gazes at her feeling a sense of regret and understanding. He sighed and ran a hand through his hair, a sign of his internal struggle.

"Bethesda, I'm sorry. I know I've been putting it off, and it's not fair to you or Gabriel. The truth is, I've been hesitant because of my strained relationship with my father. It's difficult for me to confront that pain and face the potential judgment."

But Daniel was not truthful. He carried a weighty secret, fearful that someone might eventually reveal his hidden struggle to Bethesda. The prospect of her learning the truth left him with a lingering sense of dread and uncertainty.

Bethesda's heart ached for Daniel, realizing the weight of his unresolved emotions.

"I understand, Daniel. I know it's not easy for you, and I don't want to force you into anything. But I believe that healing and rebuilding those connections can bring so much happiness and growth for all of us."

Daniel agreed with Bethesda, though a trace of apprehension still lingered within him.

"You make a valid point, Bethesda. I don't want Gabriel to miss out on the opportunity of knowing his grandparents, and I certainly don't want to deny them the joy of being part of his life. I'll push myself to push past my reservations and begin making plans for us to visit them in the near future.

"Hearing this brought hope to know that Gabriel will soon get to meet his grandparents.

"Thank you, Daniel for taking this step. This has been my prayer."

In the warmth of their embrace, Bethesda felt a renewed sense of optimism. Finally the gap between families would be repaired.She was proud of herself for taking the initiative to confront Daniel.

Yet, she firmly believed that by embracing transparency and collaborating, they could shape a future where Gabriel would be surrounded by the love and presence of both sides of his family.

VOICES OF WOMEN

While going through a rough marriage, I made up my mind to file for divorce. Little did I know that two weeks before my divorce was final, my marriage was going to be restored.

During that time, I kept asking myself "What did I just do"? After all the hurt I have been through, I am back in the same situation. The betrayal, and the unending deceit seemed insurmountable. I just couldn't understand.

One day, I felt drawn to seek God. A friend invited me to his church, giving me only a vague idea of its location. Upon finding the first church on the mentioned street, I said, "This must be it." Though it turned out not to be my friend's church, I was welcomed into a vibrant, spirit-filled church that became my sanctuary. God had other plans for me.

Even as old problems resurfaced, my new relationship with Jesus offered me a solace I'd never felt before. My husband, noticing this change, grew curious. To my surprise, one day, he showed up beside me at church. I asked him "What are you doing here? He did not reply.

In that service, a guest minister delivered a message directly to our hearts. He did not know me; I did not know him.

During the service, he called my husband and me out. He told me, not knowing what I was going through, "You have to forgive him." I knew then that God was in the midst. I must say that acknowledging the pain was hard. My husband gave his heart also to the Lord. While our marriage is far from flawless, it is rooted in the love and guidance of God. As the years went by, our bond strengthened, and today, we celebrate 43 years of shared life and faith.

Mark 10:9 says, "Therefore, what God has joined together, let no one separate." This verse stands as a testament to our journey and the power of divine intervention.

Susie

CHAPTER 15

NO, HE DIDN'T

Along with the approaching milestone of Gabriel's second birthday, Bethesda found herself caught in a whirlwind of preparations. The absence of Gabriel's paternal grandparents, from his life, was a void she had learned to accept, despite Daniel's assurances of their future visit. While the absence was a lingering source of disappointment, she had come to terms with the reality that some things were beyond her control.

Yet, within these feelings, Bethesda's excitement was brewing for a different reason. She had eagerly started to lay the groundwork for a significant transition - a shift from being a stay-at-home mother to reentering the workforce. She was motivated by the idea of taking on a job other than motherhood and using her skills and interests in a new way. This decision had nothing to do with giving up her job as a parent. Instead, it was about recognizing that she is more than just a parent and finding happiness in different parts of her life. She loved being at home with her son, cherishing every moment spent with him, but there was also an undeniable longing for the satisfaction and growth that a profession could offer.

Now that she felt optimistic again, Bethesda started to think about how she would tell Daniel about her plans. She will say that being a good mom didn't mean she had to give up all of her dreams.

She will remind him of their agreement when she was pregnant and that Gabriel is now old enough to attend a daycare center while getting advanced in school and playing with other kids. She believed they could make this choice together and knew that open communication was necessary for the health of their relationship. Feeling sure of herself, she decided it was time to talk to Daniel.

When she told Daniel, he pretended not to recall what they'd discussed years ago and expressed concern about her returning to work. Bethesda was surprised when Daniel stared at her with a blank expression of perplexity on his face, so she started to explain her objectives, dreams, and precise plans.

She expressed her eagerness to return to work and how it would boost the family's income while allowing her to progress professionally. She went on to say that she had meticulously prepared the transfer details, including childcare options and flexible work hours, as well as a plan to structure her job schedule so that she could spend as much time as possible with her family – for example, devoting some days to Gabriel and others to her career.

She noted other working women she knew who could balance work and family life by creating ways to fulfill their responsibilities without sacrificing either. She concluded that this was the most excellent way to keep the family stable while allowing her independence.

When Bethesda pressed Daniel for an answer, he pretended to be talking about something else. When she asked him what he thought, he gave her vague answers or switched to other topics.

Bethesda, "I think it's great that you have goals and plans, but I have accepted a position in another state, and we really should focus on making that trip to see my parents as soon as possible. I know you've been wanting to see them for a long time. After that, we could travel to see your family and friends."

Her voice sank in amazement and shock. She immediately asked herself, "Is what I just heard true, or is this a dream?"

Her thoughts raced as she tried to grasp this surprising information. "Wait a minute, you made this decision without even discussing it with me?"

"Yes Bethesda, I didn't think I needed to talk about my work changes or our financial future with you first. I accepted it because it would be a terrific financial opportunity for us and would greatly assist with our plans."

Bethesda's face became perplexed as she pressed him for an answer. "Moving will mean that we will be separated from our support system. Isolated from friends and family. Did you think about who we should call in an emergency? What are we going to do with Gabriel? Daniel, this decision does not sit well with me. And, by the way, what plans are you referring to?"

Because she is determined to get to the bottom of it, Daniel's attempt to derail the subject fails. "What plans are you referring to, Daniel?"

Daniel becomes apprehensive and attempts to change the subject once more. "You know, just things we've discussed before like improving our future and traveling.

" Daniel, improving our future and possibly traveling more is not an answer. I'm curious about what you're thinking."

As he shifts uneasily, Daniel's evasiveness becomes increasingly apparent. "Let's not get too caught up in this, Bethesda. We've got a lot to get done if we're going to see our folks. Maybe we may linger a bit longer by the sea and get some rest."

As she interrupts him, Bethesda's tolerance is growing thin. "No way, Daniel. This is not something to dismiss. We must communicate honestly about these issues."

He let out a sigh and turned away from her.

"Bethesda, listen carefully. I want nothing more than for you to be happy. You shouldn't go back to work now. I'll take care of everything so that you and our son don't have to worry. Give yourself a little more time, sweetheart, to get used to being a mom. Seeing how much Gabriel loves having you around during the day warms my heart so much."

But he wasn't telling her the truth; he had to stop her from going after her plans to protect his own.

She had a feeling that something was up and she was getting more and more angry, but she didn't lose her temper.

"I know you're a good provider, Daniel, but I've given it a lot of thought, and I think it is time for me to get back out there. And besides, this was our agreement. In this case, I need your help and honesty, not your lying."

Bethesda took a deep breath and told him she loved him and that they had to make decisions together in life. She began to encourage him to talk about his thoughts and worries.

Before opening up he thought of a way to stop Bethesda from carrying out her plan and keep her at home since he knew she wouldn't change her mind. Bethesda listened carefully to Daniel's calm voice. But what he said next was a surprise, and it made Bethesda worry. Her stomach got knotted, and worry grabbed at her thoughts all while she struggled to keep up with what he was saying.

Then, as Daniel kept talking, the truth came crashing down on her like a wave. He wanted another kid. She was stunned. He couldn't have been thinking about this, he couldn't have. Her carefully made plans and hopes of going back to work now seemed to be in danger. She told herself, "I'll never do that again." The possibility of having another child could have changed her plans and put her goals on hold for years.

When Bethesda heard Daniel's plea and thought back to how they had talked before, she was upset and angry. She couldn't understand why he wanted a second child but didn't care much about their first kid. When she thought about all of the reasons he had given for not spending time with Gabriel, she couldn't help but feel upset.

Daniel always put work first, was always tired, or just didn't want to spend time with their kid. It hurt her to see that he didn't care about their child, especially since she wanted those close, bonding times.

Although she felt he was neglected by his father, her love for Gabriel never changed. She had given their son all she had, and it would have made her happy to see him have a strong family bond with both parents. But because Daniel wasn't there, she felt like she was the only one taking care of their child.

As this talk went on, Bethesda's feelings were all over the place. Her future looked like it was on the edge of a cliff, and she struggled to stay true to her goals while protecting her child's mental balance.

In the middle of this fight with herself, she felt a strange mix of confusion and anger. Underneath it all, there was a strong feeling of loss. It felt like her wants were being ignored and pushed to the back of the line. This made her feel confused and like she didn't matter.

She paused for a bit to gather her thoughts before responding.

She could see things through Daniel's eyes and realized that, as an only child, he valued having additional brothers. On the other side, she was an only child and did well. But she also thought it was necessary to express her desires.

Bethesda was firm but kind when she told Daniel how she felt. She told him that she could understand why he was worried but that she had always been clear about her hopes and dreams. She told him how much she loved her job and how it made her feel good about herself. She drew attention to the fact that they had a deal, which she kept. Now he wants her to get pregnant again. How does this make sense to her? She believed something was terribly wrong with him, but what?

CHAPTER 16

REVELATIONS MET WITH DENIAL

The weight of Daniel's behavior and the strain it placed on their relationship became too heavy for Bethesda to bear. She knew that in order to truly understand and support Daniel, she needed to seek out more information about his past and the complexities of his strained relationship with his father. With a determined resolve, she decided to pay a visit to Daniel's parents before they move. She asked Sarah to watch Gabriel so that she could make this visit alone, hoping they could shed some light on his hidden struggles.

The journey to Daniel's childhood home was filled with anticipation and apprehension. Bethesda's mind raced with questions, wondering what she would uncover and how it would impact their future together. As she arrived at their doorstep, she mustered the courage to face the unknown, ready to unravel the mysteries that lay beneath the surface.

Daniel's parents greeted Bethesda warmly, unaware of the true purpose of her visit. Their genuine smiles and hospitality momentarily eased her nerves. Over a cup of tea, Bethesda delved deeper into her conversation with Daniel's parents, she expressed her concern about the strained relationship between Daniel and his father.

She couldn't help but wonder how this dynamic had affected Daniel's own understanding of love, trust, and familial connections. However, to her surprise, his parents shared a different side of the story—one that revealed a wonderful bond between father and son.

With a gentle smile, Daniel's mother recounted heartwarming stories of their family's past. She spoke of the countless hours father and son had spent together, engaged in shared hobbies, deep conversations, and moments of laughter. Daniel's father, a quiet yet strong presence, had always been a source of guidance, support, and love.

As Bethesda listened to these accounts, her perspective shifted. She realized that her assumptions about the strained relationship were misguided. Instead, she learned that Daniel struggled with borderline personality disorder and it had primarily affected his relationship with his mother, as he found it challenging to navigate the intense emotions and occasional conflicts they experienced. Daniel's parents painted images of his youth and early adulthood. Each showed his struggle with mental illness and its effect on him.

On one occasion, Daniel's feelings went from very high to very low, and he often got angry and sad over things that didn't seem important. They remembered times when he got very angry quickly, which led to heated arguments, especially with his brothers, and emotional outbursts that left everyone tired and emotionally drained.

His illness also contributed to his not being able to have stable relationships. His folks said he wanted deep relationships, but he often couldn't get them because he was afraid of being alone and had trust issues. Another reason could have been that he was mean to other people.

For example, he would be really nice to a friend, but then he wouldn't want to be around that friend anymore and would treat him badly. It hurt them so much to see how hard he tried to find a balance between wanting to love and not wanting to get hurt.

Bethesda thought they had exposed everything there was to know about the man she loved until they started talking about how impulsive he was and how sometimes he did things without thinking about the effects.

His mother shared some of the decisions he made without thinking about the consequences, like buying things on the spot or taking risks, which his therapist said revealed his inner thoughts. They often had to step in and assist him in making better, more thought-out decisions a lot.

By hearing this she became aware of his therapy and the treatment he used as an effort to manage and comprehend his disease. Despite the fact that he never accepted that he had this sickness, he continued the routine while living with his parents. However, after Daniel left home, he stopped therapy and taking his medication, ignoring his therapist and parents advising him not to, claiming that he no longer required it.

Through these stories, Bethesda learned more about Daniel's life and the storm of feelings he had to deal with. She could understand how hard it was for his parents to help and understand their son. It became clear that their journey had been filled with times of despair as they tried to figure out how to deal with Daniel's complicated emotions.

The revelations were shocking and overwhelming for Bethesda. She couldn't help but feel a whirlwind of emotions—dissappointed because of his lies yet compassion for his pain, empathy for his parents' struggle, and a deep longing to provide the love and stability he so desperately needed.

Through tears and heartfelt discussions, Bethesda discovered that Daniel's diagnosis of borderline personality disorder had shaped much of his life. It explained the intense mood swings, fear of abandonment, and the challenges he faced in forming stable relationships.

Bethesda's heart ached for Daniel, realizing the depth of his internal battle that he had kept hidden for so long. She recognized the immense courage he possessed to face each day with the weight of his disorder on his shoulders.

In that moment, Bethesda's purpose became clear. She was determined to stand by Daniel's side, to be his anchor during the storms, and to provide the love and understanding he had longed for throughout his life. She understood that she will have to be mindful of the rollercoaster ride that she will have to take but she felt that she was had the resilence to endure whatever comes her way.

The environment was so immersed with information that Bethesda soaked up everything she heard to help her understand Daniel that she lost track of time. Looking at her watch she realize that he will arrive before she return. But as she drive away from her inlaws house, she had a new way of looking at things.

She saw Daniel differently, with more understanding and a strong desire to make sure their family was cared for and safe. Armed with knowledge and kindness, she thought they would be able to face the challenges of borderline personality disorder head-on. She hoped that love and understanding would guide them through the darkest moments.

When she arrived home, Daniel car was in the driveway. She was anxious to greet him and hope that her telling him that which she knew would lift a heavy burden off of his shoulders knowing that he does not have to walk this alone.

As Bethesda entered the house, she felt Daniel's withdrawn demeanor. She could sense the heavy burden he carried, and she was eager to share the truth she had discovered in hopes of offering him comfort and support. However, as she tried to approach him with a loving kiss and a hug, he refused her affection. Her anxiety grew as she noticed the dark cloud that seemed to overshadow the atmosphere in the living room. It was evident that something was deeply troubling Daniel, and she couldn't help but feel a little concern at his rejection of her loving action.

Daniel, what's wrong?" Bethesda asked gently, trying to keep her voice steady despite her own emotions swirling within her. She took a seat beside him, her heart aching to understand the reason behind his distance.

Daniel hesitated for a moment before finally speaking, trying to control the pain he was feeling inside. "I... I just need some space right now," he muttered, avoiding eye contact.

Concerned, Bethesda held his hand, gently urging him to share what was troubling him. She reassured him that she was there to support him, no matter what he was going through.

He takes a moment, trying to control the frustration he's feeling, " I came home from work, and you weren't here. Where were you and where is Gabriel? You did not tell me you were going out today."

She remembered her conversation with his parents as well as his frustration. "I'm sorry, Daniel. I should have let you know where I was going. It was thoughtless of me to not leave any information."

Daniel runs a hand through his hair, clearly upset. "It's not just about leaving a note. We should communicate about these things. We're living together, and it's important for me to know when you are going out. You still did not answer my question."

"I went to see your parents today," she began, her voice soft and tender. "They told me about your struggles, Daniel. I know about the depression and emotional instability you've been facing. You don't have to carry this burden alone."

"My parents!"

Daniel's was surprised, and he seemed to wrestle with his emotions. As Bethesda continue sharing what she had learned from Daniel's parents, his initial surprise gave way to an unexpected outburst of anger. His face contorted with rage, and he accused her of betraying him and accepting lies about him without his consent.

The more she tried to explain that her intention was to understand him better and improve their communication, the more his aggression intensified.

"Why would you go behind my back like this?!"

Daniel's voice boomed, his fists clenched tightly. "The Bible tells you that you have to be submissive to me. I am the man and make the decisions. What don't you understand about this? How can you say you are a woman of God and not obey? I trusted you, and now you're throwing lies and hearsay in my face!"

Feeling the weight of his accusations, Bethesda keep her composure during the escalating tension.

"Daniel, I didn't mean to betray your trust. I understand your position as the decision maker but I only wanted to understand what was going on so we could work through this together," she responded calmly, hoping to defuse the situation.

But her attempt to explain only seemed to fuel his anger further. He retorted with bitter words, questioning her loyalty and claiming she had no right to interfere in his private struggles. As his anger grew, so did the rift between them, leaving Bethesda feeling hurt and deeply misunderstood.

"Stop trying to play the Savior! You have no idea what I'm going through," Daniel snapped, his face flushed with emotion.

"You think you can fix everything, but you can't because there is nothing wrong with me! You are the one who needs to be fixed. The problem is you."

She never wanted to be his Savior; she simply wanted to support him and share their burdens as partners. Yet, Daniel seemed unable to see her intentions clearly.

"I'm not trying to fix you, Daniel. I just want to be there for you, to understand you better," she replied softly, her voice quivering with emotion. "I love you, and I want to help you through this difficult time."

But her attempts to reach him seemed to fall on deaf ears as Daniel continued to lash out in anger.

"I am tired of people and their speculations, and that's to include you! " and he bolted out of the house like a wildhorse trying to avoid being captured.

The frustration of feeling misunderstood and dismissed built up within Bethesda, but she knew that responding with anger would only escalate the situation further. With a heavy heart, Bethesda chose to take a step back, giving Daniel the space he seemed to need. She hoped that with time, he would be able to see her intentions more clearly and recognize her support.

Bethesda went into another room with tears on her cheeks because Daniel's anger and violence were so strong that they scared her. She felt the pain of Daniel's words cut through her heart like a sharp blade, ripping it so deeply to the core that even the best cardiologist would not be able to fix it.

At that moment, it seemed like a part of her broke, leaving her feeling exposed and emotionally raw as her heart hurt and she tried to figure out how they had gotten to this painful place. Daniel didn't look like the loving and caring partner she had known.

Instead, he looked like a stranger. She had seen him angry before, but never this way. The image of the loving and caring partner she had known seemed to blur, replaced by a version of Daniel unfamiliar to her. She had seen him upset but never like this.

This emotional turmoil had caught her off guard which made her worry that she might not be able to help him. It was a heart-wrenching realization that healing couldn't occur if he refused to acknowledge his struggles and accept the support she offered.

Her tears were her only solace for dealing with Daniel's rage and accusations. She had always been sure that they loved each other, and she never changed her mind. Still, she didn't know why, but his sharp words hurt her and made her question everything she thought she knew about their relationship.

"You are the one who needs to be fixed. "The problem is you," the voice kept tormenting her and bringing her to the conclusion that her actions and intentions caused the break in their relationship. After hours of struggling with the mocking voice in her brain that had left her physically and mentally exhausted, she recalls the verse that says her heavenly Father will not put more on her than she can handle, and when it becomes too much, He will provide an escape route.

Gaining inward strength, a little echo vibrated from her lips as she screamed for aid from the merciless storm that had suddenly descended on her, leaving her defenseless.

She immediately felt a wave of tranquility, allowing her to contain her emotions and focus on herself. Despite her broken heart, she vowed to be kind to herself and allow herself to process her pain. She wiped away her tears, knowing she needed to give herself and Daniel space to digest their emotions.

Even though she was uncertain, Bethesda tried to find comfort in the love she still had for him. She knew that their relationship was strong, but it seemed to be getting weaker at the moment.

This dark cloud hung over them while she tried to put the pieces of her heart back together and deal with the insecurity of their future. She wanted so much to hold on to a little bit of hope and pray that love would win and that their journey to healing could start at some point. But for now, she must protect herself.

VOICES OF WOMEN

When a man finds a wife, he finds a good thing and obtains favor from the Lord, which means several different things.

First, to find something, you must be in search of it. In order to find a wife, a man has to have settled in his mind; that's what he's looking for. Not casual dating, but rather dating with a purpose.

The second thought that comes to mind is that God said that when he found a wife, he had found a good thing. He didn't say when a man finds a woman. He clearly stated when a man finds a wife, which tells me wife is not just gender-specific but rather character-specific. Thereby reminding me of the virtuous woman attributes detailed in Proverbs 31. Once a man finds a woman with wifely characteristics, he obtains favor from the Lord! Why? Because this would later prove to be an outward example of God and his church. Therefore, favor abounds because there is no greater love.

Thirdly, it did not say that when a wife finds her husband's favor, it is begotten. There are many reasons for this. Chiefly because a man must first be a man to recognize a wife! I knew when I was dating my now-husband that he was my husband. Way before he knew. But I never pressured him or asked the question about marriage. Not once.

We dated for 7 years. Why did it take so long? He had to become the man who was then mature enough and settled in his mind to be looking for a wife, and seven years later that day came. Now, I wouldn't dare tell any of the readers to wait seven years, but in my case, we have made so many advancements together over the years.

We would sit and have Bible study together while we were datin dating :). So yes, I knew he was the one. But it wasn't my place to tell him. He had to recognize that good thing to make a forever commitment. Rushing a boy to be a man leads to disaster and a life not pleasing to God and more specifically representative of Him and His church!

Fourth, once the two have connected, favor is released that simply. Therefore, it is not up to you to change your person, belittle your person, disrespect your person, or rule over your person. It tampers with your favor, much like what we saw in the story of Daniel and Bethesda.

Fifth, there is a responsibility that comes along with being a husband and then a wife. Desirable? Yes! But work? Most definitely. And our reward? FAVOUR! And oh, how good it is to live a life of companionship and love sprinkled with favor.

Danna Tyler

CHAPTER 17

DR. JEKYLL OR MR. HYDE

For two long, agonizing weeks, Daniel's behavior had undergone a drastic transformation, leaving Bethesda dealing with the duality of his personality. Like Dr. Jekyll and Mr. Hyde, his actions veered between tender love and emotional connection to cold indifference and rejection. The distance he kept from her and Gabriel seemed to rip her apart as she felt the weight of his psychological retreat crushing her soul.

During those difficult weeks, Bethesda tried everything she could think of to reach out to Daniel, desperate to regain his love and acceptance. She prepared his favorite meals, hoping to remind him of the cherished moments they had shared around the dinner table.

But he refused to eat the food, pushing it away with a cold and distant gaze.

She decorated their home with pictures of their family, hoping that the memories they held would stir something within him. But Daniel remained unresponsive, seemingly immune to the sentiments captured in those photographs.

Bethesda tried to engage him in conversation to coax out the emotions that seemed locked away within him. But every attempt was met with silence or brief responses, leaving her feeling shut out and isolated. All of her efforts were in vain and the man she loved seemed unreachable, lost within the depths of his own turmoil.

Finally, on a day when she couldn't endure any longer, she got the courage to confront him with her deepest concern. She looked into his eyes, her voice quivering with emotion as she declared, "I love you, Daniel, and I will do anything to make this family whole again. If that means giving up my career and having another child to make sure Gabriel does not have to experience what you did - although she knew he was lying - when you're ready, I'll do it. But please, let us find our way back to each other."

The air seemed to crack as Daniel's eyes locked with hers. For a moment, it seemed as though the emotional fortress he had built around himself might crumble. The battle between Dr. Jekyll and Mr. Hyde played out on his face as he wrestled with his feelings and his fears.

Finally, after what felt like an eternity, he spoke, his voice raw with emotion.

"Bethesda, I don't want you to give up your dreams for me. But I've been feeling lost and broken inside, and I didn't know how to reach out. I'm scared that you'll leave me if you see this side of me, so I pushed you away."

Sadness overwhelm her as she reached out and took his hand in hers. "I won't leave you, Daniel," she said softly. "We're in this together, and I'm here to support you, no matter what."

With that admission, a weight seemed to lift from Daniel's shoulders, and the emotional walls he had built began to fall. He allowed himself to be vulnerable, to share the pain and struggles he had kept hidden for so long.

At that moment, Bethesda saw hope, but she still thought the period of insecurity and turbulent emotions was far from over, even though she knew they had a new sense of understanding and connection.

Their tears mixed as they hugged each other, and Bethesda knew the road ahead would be rough. She would have to be on the lookout to see if Dr. Jekyll or Mr. Hyde showed up. She knew she would regret giving in to his request, but it was worth it to get close to him emotionally and then intimately later that night.

As the sun rose on a new day, the atmosphere seemed to have shifted, carrying with it a sense of renewal and hope. Bethesda woke up to the refreshing aroma of breakfast being prepared in the kitchen. Her heart skipped a beat as she realized that Daniel was taking the initiative to make her morning special. He had gotten Gabriel ready for the day and was now preparing breakfast in bed for her before he left for work.

As she walked into the kitchen, she was greeted by a warm smile and a kiss. The weight of the past weeks seemed to have lifted, replaced by a newfound sense of love and connection. Bethesda was grateful as she sat down to enjoy the thoughtful breakfast he had prepared.

Throughout their breakfast, they exchanged affectionate glances and gentle touches, rebuilding the emotional intimacy they had feared lost. Bethesda cherished these moments, realizing that healing was an ongoing process, and that their love could weather the storms that life threw their way.

Later that day, while she was lost in the peaceful moments with her thoughts, a text message from Daniel interrupted her daydreaming.

The message read, "Go outside. I have a surprise for you."

Curious and excited, Bethesda made her way to the front door. As she stepped outside, she couldn't believe her eyes. There, in the driveway, was a beautiful car adorned with a big purple bow, and her name written in large letters on the windshield. Both feelings of suspicion and happiness by Daniel's thoughtful gesture, she saw him step out from behind the car, grinning with pride, tears of joy began to roll down her cheeks.

He ran over and sweep her off of her feet and said, "I want you to know how much I love you," with words of sincerity.

There was an instantaneous wave of affection and appreciation for him. Finally Bethesda felt the love that she longed for radiating within her. She realized as they embraced that the future might not be as challenging as she speculated because they were now together. Although she had to put her career on hold again, she beleive that another opportunity will come again. But for now she visualizing the car in the driveway as a reminder of the endless possibilities that awaits them on the road of a brighter tomorrow.

CHAPTER 18

HIDDEN SUFFERING

After getting Gabriel settled for the day, Bethesda struggled to adjust to her new normal as her secret pain bore heavily on her. Despite the turbulence in her head, she sought ways to find joy in even the most mundane activities.

Previously vibrant and ambitious, she now appears to be surrounded by a cloud of sorrow. The car in the driveway no longer represents their enduring love, steadfast support, and limitless potential. She secretly regrets not having the freedom to choose her path in life.

Although the strong bond they had two months ago is slowly eroding, a fragile peace that attempted to mend the cracks in their relationship arose due to Daniel's apparent progress with his challenges. The calm that had followed his apparent recovery from his last episode was a relief. However, the calm seemed welcoming on the surface, despite the unspoken pain that needed to be handled within.

Bethesda hopes that Daniel's efforts to spend quality time with Gabriel are a sign that their family life is improving, and this gives them a renewed sense of security.

Daniel tried to prioritize their connection to demonstrate his dedication to their healing process. In an effort to reignite the flame that had dimmed due to the challenges they were facing, he made sure they had a date night every week. He put work aside, obviously prioritizing personal relationships over professional obligations.

Outwardly, Bethesda tried to embrace this gesture as a bandage for her inner pain, hoping that it would bridge the emotional chasm between them. She masked her longing for deeper understanding and intimacy, convincing herself that these moments of connection were enough to sustain them.

But despite Daniel's efforts, the wounds within her heart remained raw and unattended. The silence she bore became heavier with each passing day, and her heart yearned for a resolution that seemed elusive. She wondered if the surface calmness was merely a facade, a temporary illusion that veiled the deeper issues they had yet to confront.

When alone, she realizes that her deep feelings are fighting against her strong desire to escape a force that has trapped her. With every passing moment, she must fight for her freedom because she is torn between acceptance and desiring more.

As time went by quickly in front of her eyes, Bethesda turned to her area of instability for comfort. She loved going out on dates with Daniel and treasured those special times when they were close. But the pain of her quiet suffering kept coming back - a silent cry for help and understanding.

Although their home was shown as peaceful, Bethesda realized that natural healing required more than just outward gestures. She believed they were merely covering their wounds with a bandage and putting off the necessary healing, which needed honesty and openness. She couldn't help but hope that one day the environment would be filled with the warmth and calm she desired, not just as a patch but as a reminder of their shared path toward love and understanding. Until then, she was trapped in the peaceful storm of her silent suffering, waiting for the day when the agony she didn't express would be heard.

Sunday morning has arrived, and Bethesda is still in bed, which is uncommon for her because she is usually up and about before the alarm goes off. However, the alarm was blasting loudly today, and when Daniel reached over to turn it off, he realized she was still asleep and gently shook her to wake her up. Concerned, he inquired about her well-being.

Her answer was tired and weak. She said she wasn't feeling

well and asked him to take Gabriel to church since she wouldn't be going. As he left, Bethesda tried to fight off the feeling of sickness that was coming over her.

But as the morning went on, the feeling of sickness got worse, and soon she ran to the bathroom to throw up. It was scary, and she couldn't stop worrying that something very wrong might be going on.

Bethesda decided to try to make an appointment with her doctor the following day in order to hide this from Daniel until she got more information. It was fortunate that she was able to get a same-day appointment, saving her the agonizing wait.

After undergoing some tests and a thorough examination, Bethesda received news that she didn't want to hear. It wasn't enough that she was in pain and experiencing heartbreak; now her doctor had confirmed that she was pregnant. The realization hit her like a ton of bricks, leaving her conflicted and overwhelmed.

Telling Daniel would excite and delight him, but for Bethesda, it would only make her feel worse. She thought back to when things were bad between them and told him she would be open to having another child. But she was still planning to return to her job goals and plans for her path when she heard the news. It made her feel uncertain and stuck. She didn't want this to happen. The timing didn't feel right, and she knew this would hurt her plans for her job.

Her feelings were all over the place, and she felt terrible about the promises she had made to Daniel and the dreams he had. She also worried she would lose herself again as a mother, giving up her dreams and freedom.

As the news started sinking in, Bethesda was again at a crossroads. She had to decide whether to tell Daniel or find a way to handle it alone. In a time filled with uncertainty and fragility, Bethesda knew she had to find the courage to be honest with herself and her feelings. Even though she already knew what would happen, she needed to talk to Daniel about how she felt and what she feared.

As she prepared to break the news to him, she hoped that he would be able to understand her perspective and assist her in coping with the new challenges that this change of events would bring.

She spent some time with Gabriel and made sure he was comfortable in bed before going into the office to break the news. Daniel ecstatically makes the dos and don'ts list before she can finish her sentence, which she knew did not include working - even remotely. She felt an instantaneous feeling of sadness as she visualized nine months of solidarity confinement plus an additional two years.

Her broken heart left her with an overpowering sensation of loneliness and pain that made her feel like she was left to bear the weight of the world on her own. Fear and uncertainty obscured the idea of asking her loved ones for help and understanding. She hadn't seen them in a long time, and now she was cut off from the network of friends and family who had once been so essential to her survival.

As she considered how Daniel had tricked her into gradually cutting ties with them after moving away, the weight of her loneliness grew. He pressed her to spend less time with others and more time with him after first persuading her that their relationship deserved exclusive concentration. She gradually cut herself off from those who loved her the most, thinking that this was the price of their devotion. They called her frequently, but she barely spoke.

Now that she is caught in a cycle of solitude and has no one with whom to discuss her darkest thoughts, her greatest worries, or the pain she is going through, the negative effects of her decision have become apparent. She wanted a sympathetic ear and a kind heart, but the barriers Daniel had put up seemed impenetrable.

Bethesda yearned for the comfort of her loved ones, the understanding they could offer, and the knowledge that could help her find a way forward in those vulnerable moments when she wondered if her faith was strong enough to conquer the challenges that lay before her.

She was compelled to think back on her life and the depressing changes that had happened over time. As a small spark of truth inside her started to shine brightly, illuminating the warnings that had come from her friends and family, she started to realize everything she had sacrificed in order to please Daniel, losing parts of herself along the way.

On the other hand, she thought Daniel was being honest when he surprised her with a new car, spent time with Gabriel, and said he loved her from the bottom of his heart. Maybe he was finally admitting that he was having trouble and asking her for help gave her hope that things could get better. But she was feeling a storm of different emotions.

Part of her wanted to believe that Daniel was ready to face his problems and help them heal because of how open he was. But another part of her was nervous because she remembered how hurt she had been and how far apart they were from one another.

She couldn't quickly eliminate the lingering doubts because she remembered how painful it was to feel alone and abandoned when Daniel didn't show her love or care. She wasn't sure how to get better and was afraid of getting hurt again.

Her mind was full of things from the past, like signs she didn't listen to and people with whom she lost touch. She was torn between wanting to think that Daniel had changed his mind and seeing warning signs from the past.

Even though she felt a lot of different things, she knew she had to decide. Ignoring Daniel's behavior and any red flags could hurt not only their relationship but also his health. She couldn't deny that she needed help and a plan to improve.

CHAPTER 19

HANGING BY A TATTERED THREAD

Being pregnant, caring for Gabriel, and helping Daniel made Bethesda's days a never-ending struggle. Daniel kept her on an unrelenting emotional rollercoaster, leaving her grasping at a frayed thread of hope as she struggled to weather the storm.

Therefore, even though it was still a long way off, she wanted to start preparing for their new child's birth. She didn't want to endure the same last-minute rush they had with Gabriel when she had to shop online while on bedrest. When she went to the store in person, she could see all the choices and carefully plan for the baby's needs. She told Daniel about it because she wanted to discuss their budget for getting ready for the baby. But he ignored her worries and told her he had everything under control.

The transfers to Bethesda's personal account appeared to be declining over the months, leaving her with just enough money to cover her expenses. Despite this, she didn't want to worry about money because she thought Daniel was taking care of everything. But one day, she received a past-due bill in the mail, which prompted her to look into it more.

She was shocked to learn that they had racked up a sizable debt and that their financial condition was anything but steady. She questioned why Daniel hadn't been upfront with her about their finances because she felt betrayed and alarmed by the information. It soon became apparent that his excessive spending was negatively impacting their financial stability.

With the understanding of their perilous situation, she wasn't sure if she should talk to Daniel or try to solve the problem independently. She knew that if she faced the problem, it would likely lead to a fight. Still, with a baby on the way, she couldn't ignore how important it was to protect their financial future.

Now, she has to make a hard decision: Should she talk to Daniel and ask for financial openness, which could cause trouble in her marriage? Should she take things into her own hands, get help with money, and manage the family's budget?

Bethesda knew that what she chose to do would have significant effects on her family. She wanted to ensure they had a promising future, but she was also worried that talking to him about their money problems would affect their already shaky relationship.

When things were unclear, Bethesda reminded herself of how strong she had become over the years. She had been through many storms and came out of each one stronger. She knew she couldn't ignore the truth and that the only way to move forward was to face their money problems head-on.

But instead of taking responsibility for what he did, Daniel blamed his boss, who he said hadn't given him the raise when he had asked. He also tried to make her feel bad by saying that every time he turned around, she was always asking for money.

Even though she was starting to show, she suggested working part-time to help pay the bill and return the car he had just bought for her. She was surprised by how angry and defensive Daniel was. He immediately turned down her offer and asked her if she didn't trust him with the money. He snapped at her, saying that he could handle the problem on his own and that it was his job to take care of them.

She tried to explain that it wasn't because she didn't trust him but because she wanted to find a way for them to share the load. She wanted to be a part of their financial journey because she thought that if they worked as a team, they could solve their problems faster.

But Daniel's pride seemed to be an unbreakable wall that stopped any efforts to bring them closer together. The fact that he refused to return the car he had bought for her also added to her depression. It was a sign of his love and care, but she couldn't get rid of the feeling that it also was a financial burden.

When Bethesda saw that her efforts to help and make a difference weren't appreciated, her heart sank. She didn't doubt his abilities; she just wanted to support their family in any way she could. But at that moment, it seemed like all her efforts were for nothing, and she felt rejected and helpless.

She couldn't help but think that maybe he wasn't as kind as she had thought. His answer came from pride and a desire to control their money. When they were together, Bethesda often felt that her opinion was not taken seriously.

Daniel seemed to see her more as someone who could help him than as a real partner who could bring her skills and ideas to the table. Their relationship felt like a delicate dance, with each step full of stress and doubt. She wondered if there was a way to get around the things that were getting in the way and find a middle ground to work together to solve their money problems. The resistance to her offer left her feeling like her efforts to help and support him were not valued. It was as if he wanted to keep the reins of their financial affairs firmly in his hands, unwilling to relinquish any control or share the responsibility.

It also got more challenging for her to manage their problems as Daniel started acting out more frequently and displaying excessive, inappropriate wrath that would flare up at the slightest provocation. She was constantly living on the edge because she had no idea when his anger would erupt, which was extremely draining on her emotions.

One night, they went out to dinner to try to get away from their worries. But even this seemingly simple trip turned out to be complicated. Daniel didn't want to wait while their waiteress talked to another customer, so he kept trying to get her attention. Bethesda tried to talk to him by telling him that the server would join them as soon as she could.

However, Daniel's rage burst like a volcano when the server finally arrived to offer assistance. He attacked her angrily, blaming her for the hold-up, and set off a spectacle that had everyone in the vicinity gasping in disbelief. Bethesda made every effort to calm him down, but he seemed unable to control his anger and pushed her against the wall, causing her to fall. As another customer called 911, an older man jumped up to help her get up from the floor. As other guests watched this happen, Bethesda felt humiliated and ashamed.

Daniel put some cash on the table, forcefully grabbed her hand, and said, "Let's go."

When he got to the car, he pushed her through the driver's door to the passenger side, got in, and drove away. Daniel's bad behavior ruined the evening, but thankfully, when they got home, Gabriel was already asleep. After the sitter departed, Bethesda told Daniel she wasn't feeling well. He decided to take a shower and go to bed, telling her she shouldn't try to take his place as the man because he knew what he was doing.

When she awoke the following morning, the house was quiet because he had already left for work and had dropped Gabriel off at school. Still in bed, she thought about the terrible thing that took place last night.

In the thick of it all, Bethesda felt caught between how much she loved him and how much she needed to protect herself from the mental and physical attack. She wanted to help and be there for him when he was having trouble, but it was clear that it hurt her health.

Now that her mother and friends know she is pregnant, they call her more often out of worry and want to see her because it has been a while since they lived in the same state. As usual, she makes up reasons why they can't come out to visit and tells them about a life that has nothing to do with the real world. Feeling the weight of this isolation, she finds herself alone, lying beside the pool of hope, waiting for someone to come and help her get in.

This sense of abandonment is amplified since Daniel, who she thought was her knight in shining armor, is no longer there to offer his support. She can see the issues from the last several years with her beside the pool.

A terrible force is also pursuing her, mocking her, and trying to persuade her that the person she once was is not someone she will ever be again. She must consequently stop trying and give up. Never again will she be able to improve herself. It also tells her that Daniel's problem was because she wasn't happy with being a mother and wife.

She frantically clung to the thread of hope that was frayed and worn, believing that one day she would get the support and understanding needed to guide her on a path to repair. She attempted to stay calm despite the upsetting effects of Daniel's condition, but the reality of her predicament appeared to get worse with each passing day, and she couldn't help but wonder if they were both hanging by a thread.

Later that day, the stress and tension became too much for her. She collapsed and fell downstairs while attempting to carry the laundry to the washroom. Monday was her washday, and Daniel always made sure the laundry was downstairs; however, still upset from what happened the night before, he decided she should do it since she wanted to be the man.

Fortunately, Gabriel's school had notified Daniel that she had not arrived to pick up the boy, so he went home right away. Feeling panicked and worried as he entered the house, he called out to her, only to find her unconscious in a puddle of blood at the foot of the stairs, with dirty clothing all around her. His heart rate increased, and he immediately dialed 911 for help.

Daniel clung to Bethesda until the ambulance arrived. He prayed for her survival. When he caught a glimpse of what he had put her through, he couldn't help but cry, especially because he had harmed her physically and mentally the day before.

He considers how enraged he became in the restaurant and wonders whether it made her sick. He admits that he should have carried the clothes. He gazes at her and notices the stillness on her face. He cries out to God, pleading for mercy and vowing to change his attitude toward her and his mental state from the day before.

After stabilizing her condition, the medical team rushed

her to the hospital for further medical care. Daniel's troubled gaze never left his face as he softly caressed her cheek inside the ambulance.

"Lord, please look after my wife," he said quietly.

He kissed her on the cheek and promised to be there for her no matter what happened next. As soon as they arrived at the hospital, the emergency staff leapt into action, attentively checking her health and working to provide the best care possible.

In this awful moment, Daniel was torn between his fears and responsibilities. He dreaded the thought of reaching out to their families and friends, not wanting to expose his own dark secret. But deep down, he recognized the seriousness of the situation and knew that he could not keep the truth hidden. He contemplated calling, but decided to pray for a miracle to take place instead.

After several hours, the doctor arrived to give Daniel an update on her status. He states that they did all possible to save her life, including surgery to stop the bleeding caused by a catastrophic injury she had sustained, and that she should be conscious shortly. As the doctor proceeded to speak, Daniel's heart sank.

"I'm sorry to inform you," the doctor stated seriously, "that despite our best efforts, the baby did not survive."

He further stressed that her recovery would require his continual presence with her, especially in light of the devastating news that she had lost the baby. Those words lingered in the air, reminding Daniel of the harsh reality he had to face. He was overcome with feelings ranging from anguish for his child's death to anxiety for Bethesda's well-being. Nevertheless, Daniel was determined to be there for her when she needed him the most.

He sat there staring at her for hours, unsure what to do. Because he knows Gabriel is secure, all he wants to hear from the doctor is good news about her condition. If she wakes up from her coma, he will avoid having to contact her family.

She was still unconscious when the doctor arrived to check on her. He promised Daniel that they would keep an eye on her and hoped she would recover soon. But if she doesn't, they'll have to discuss other options.

Despite hearing what the doctor said, Daniel was not satisfied with simply allowing her to remain in her current state. He was curious whether there was anything they could do to help her get out of this situation sooner. Recognizing his concern, the doctor assures him that this is the best option for the time being and promises to return tomorrow.

Daniel's great hopes that the news would be favorable to him had been crushed. His anxiety level now climbs with each tick of the clock on the wall, which appears to irritate him rather than help. He couldn't put off calling any longer, so he left the room to call them while the nurse checked her vital signs.

As he walks down the hall, worried, he finds a quiet spot, takes a deep breath, and looks at his phone and says to himself,

"This is important, and I need to make this call."

Suddenly, he hears Bethesda friend Sarah say, "He was never good for her, and she deserved better. Why did they get married?"

Next, her father chimed in on the conversation. "I knew this would happen. He isn't reliable enough to take care of a family."

Then her mother adds to what his mind is thinking: "And now she has to pay for his carelessness. He never took care of her while she was pregnant before, so what makes us think that he would do anything different this time around?"

He closes his eyes briefly and grips the phone tightly as he struggles to push those thoughts away.

"No, I can't give in to those voices. I have to be brave for her."

Sarah's voice persistently nags at his mind. "You can't hide your secrets forever, Daniel."

Daniel exhales deeply and starts to dial his in-laws number. Before the line connected, he heard a frantic call coming from his wife's room, forcing him to hurriedly disconnect the connection and run back to her. The nurse speaks urgently as he enters the room.

"Mr. Johnson, she's awake and stable. We're only discussing how she's doing."

Daniel's eyes widen in amazement as he notices Bethesda sitting up and talking with the nurse.

Bethesda gives him a weak but relieved smile. "Daniel, you're here."

He goes to her side and lovingly embraces her.

"This is amazing. Thank God you're finally awake," he says as he kisses her on the cheek. "Baby, I will always be here. I will never leave your side. I was so worried about you."

Bethesda looks at him with concern and asks, "What happened? Why am I in the hospital?" Daniel pauses for a moment, takes a deep breath, and looks into her eyes with reassurance. Sweetheart, you fell down the stairs and were in a coma for a while. But the fact that you're awake now is all that matters. Daniel takes her hand in his and rubs it against his cheek.

"I've been frightened and confused without you. I am so sorry for the way I have treated you and promise to change. Bethesda, you are my beloved. I'm relieved you're okay."

She wrinkles her brows, trying to remember the incident. Then suddenly she pulls her hand away, her face solemn.

"What about our child, Daniel? What happened to Grace? How's Grace?"

He forced a hard swallow and cleared his throat in response to the questions. "Grace, she... um, Bethesda, we lost the baby. I'm so sorry. It's been really tough on you. I should have been more considerate. I let you down."

Her eyes fill with tears as she processes the information, her voice quivering. "Grace, our baby girl..."

Silence overshadowed the room, and the sound of the clock was no longer heard. Bethesda was speechless as she stared into the unknown.

VOICES OF WOMEN

Finding a wife is a blessing and a sign of God's favor. Every woman deserves to be cherished, adored, and deeply loved. In a relationship, never allow complacency to set in, for taking one another for granted can erode the foundation of a marriage. As God decrees in Ephesians 5:25, "Husbands, love your wives, just as Christ loved the church and gave himself up for her." The love a husband should have for his wife is profound and divine.

In moments of vulnerability, when a wife seeks comfort and a shoulder to cry on, her husband should be there, steadfast and supportive. Avoid inflicting pain, whether intentional or unintentional, and when disagreements arise, address them head-on. Ignoring issues or brushing them aside can lead to bigger problems down the road, akin to tripping over an obstacle you've ignored. While words of love are beautiful, actions carry more weight and truth. As a reminder, Galatians 6:7 says, "Do not be deceived: God cannot be mocked. A man reaps what he sows."

A thriving marriage is built on pillars of love, trust, commitment, and mutual respect. Trust is the foundation; without it, the relationship stands on shaky ground. Transparency and honesty are crucial – admit your mistakes to one another, ensuring the bond between you strengthens and grows. Lies and deceit can shatter the sanctity of your union, preventing it from flourishing. Above all, keeping God at the center of your marriage will guide and anchor you both through life's challenges.

Warmly,
Claressa

CHAPTER 20

MY AWAKENING

The weight of Grace's death hit them both like a tidal wave, leaving them searching for consolation and understanding. Bethesda and Daniel clung to Gabriel and each other in their shared pain. They frequently console Gabriel when he talks and asks questions about his sister, knowing that one day he will accept her absence from his life. They also acknowledged the importance of confronting the difficulties they had avoided for so long. It was a wake-up call, a bitter reminder of how much their problems had cost them both.

As they battled with the excruciating aftermath of the loss, they began to open up to each other, revealing their concerns, hopes, and vulnerabilities. It was a difficult road, but they were traveling it together, learning to rely on one another for support and understanding. However, Bethesda, on the other hand, continued to navigate the emotional storm, unable to escape her feeling that their relationship was imbalanced.

With regret and sorrow, Bethesda sat in the living room across from Daniel. She had hoped that the tragedy of baby Grace's miscarriage would bring them closer together, but instead, it seemed to have driven them further apart. Daniel's emotional state had worsened, and she knew that both of them needed professional help to navigate the storm that was tearing them apart.

"Daniel," her voice trembling with emotion, said, "We can't keep going on like this. Your constant verbal attacks are tearing us apart. We need therapy, both for ourselves and for our relationship."

Daniel looked at her, his expression hardening, and replied, "I don't need therapy, and I don't see why you think it's necessary. I'm the man of this household, and the Bible tells you to be submissive to me. I make the decisions, and you should just trust in that."

Bethesda felt a lump form in her throat as she listened to his words. The pain of his dismissive attitude and his use of the Bible to keep her trapped weighed heavily on her heart. She had always valued her faith, but she couldn't shake the feeling that he was using it as a means to control her.

"Dani," she said, her voice quivering, "I believe in the principles of the Bible, but I also believe in mutual respect and understanding in a relationship. We're supposed to be partners, supporting each other and making decisions together. It's not about who is submissive to whom; it's about working as a team."

Daniel's eyes narrowed, and his voice grew sharper as he retorted, "Well, maybe you just don't understand the true meaning of submission. It's about accepting my authority and letting me lead our family."

"But it's not just about you leading," Bethesda pleaded, her eyes swelling up with tears. I need to be heard, to have a say in our lives too. We're both humans, both flawed, and we both need help to navigate our struggles."

"Help? What help do we need? I can handle everything on my own."

As Daniel scoffed at the suggestion of seeking help, he continued to lash out, using the painful memory of baby Grace's miscarriage as a weapon against Bethesda.

"If you had just listened to me," he sneered, "you would not have lost our baby girl. Maybe if you weren't so focused on yourself and seeking help, she would still be here."

His words were sharp, reopening the deep wounds of grief and guilt that she had been trying to heal. The weight of his accusation was too much to bear, and Bethesda felt the overwhelming weight of despair crashing down on her.

In that moment, the emotional burden she had been carrying for so long became unbearable. She couldn't keep it all inside anymore. With an anguished cry, she collapsed to the floor, her sobs echoing through the room.

But instead of offering comfort or remorse, Daniel's response was callous and indifferent.

"Stop making a scene," he said coldly, his voice devoid of empathy. "You brought this on yourself by not listening to me."

His words only fueled her pain, leaving her feeling isolated and trapped in her suffering. The emotional abuse he inflicted on her was relentless, and she felt like she had no escape from his manipulation.

As Bethesda's heart broke, she realized that she couldn't bear this burden alone any longer. She needed help, support, and understanding. She needed to find the strength to break free from the emotional chains that bound her to this toxic relationship.

Through her tears, she made a silent vow to herself—she would no longer allow Daniel's hurtful words to define her worth or dictate her actions. As she struggled to pick herself up, she was determined to find the strength to rise above the pain and take the steps towards reclaiming her life and her happiness.

Bethesda took a deep breath, trying to steady herself. "I love you, Daniel, and I want us to get better. But we can't do that if we keep pushing each other away. Please, let's consider therapy for both of us. I want to heal together and find a way to be happy again."

Daniel looked away, his jaw tensing, but he didn't respond. Bethesda's heart sank as she realized that he wasn't ready to face his own demons, and he wasn't willing to let her be part of his healing journey. In that moment, she knew that she had to take care of herself, even if it meant making difficult decisions. She couldn't allow herself to continue in the rut of despair any longer.

With tears streaming down her cheeks, she mustered the strength to tell him, "If you won't seek help, then I will find a way to heal without you."

As she left the room, a heavy silence hung in the air. Bethesda knew that it would be challenging, but she was determined to find her strength again and break free from the emotional chains that bound her.

Bethesda had grown so accustomed to the patterns of Daniel's behavior that she could sense when one of his episodes was looming on the horizon. With Gabriel no longer a little boy, she had to find creative ways to shield him from his dad's outbursts. Whether it was allowing him to watch his favorite television program or spending time with the neighbor's son, she did her best to create a safe space for him away from the storm.

Only when Daniel was at work did she feel some relief. She was able to finally relax and get some alone time. But the peace was short-lived because once he returned home, he demanded her full attention. If she dared to be preoccupied with anything else, he would immediately feign illness or distress, knowing that she would drop everything to take care of him.

It was an exhausting cycle, leaving Bethesda emotionally drained and feeling like a prisoner in her own home. The hope she once held for seeking help was slowly fading away as each episode seemed to cement the painful reality of their situation.

In her commitment to Daniel, Bethesda neglected her own needs and desires. The dreams and aspirations she once held dear seemed like distant memories, buried beneath the weight of their relationship's challenges. She had put her career on hold, sacrificing her own ambitions to be there for Daniel and their family. The toll it took on her relationship with Gabriel was heartbreaking.

She yearned to shield him from the emotional storms that raged within their home, but she could only do so much. As he grew older, he became more aware of the tensions, and Bethesda always felt bad about putting him in such an unstable environment. While she loved Gabriel and wanted to be a devoted mother, she couldn't shake the nagging feeling that a part of her was missing.

Each day that passed without progress in their relationship, the chapters of hope for a better future together closed one by one. Now she sees that the once-vibrant and independent woman she used to be is slowly fading away. The vision of a happy family and a loving partnership seemed to dim with each passing moment. Bethesda couldn't help but question if this was the life she was destined to lead, trapped in a cycle of pain and uncertainty.

She yearned for a connection where they could communicate openly and vulnerably, where they could both share their struggles and find love in each other's arms. Yet, despite her efforts, it felt like she was shouting into the void, her pleas for understanding and healing falling on deaf ears.

Along with the relentless emotional and sometimes physical abuse, it chipped away at her self-esteem, leaving her feeling diminished and trapped in her circumstances.

Despite her inner turmoil, Bethesda's love for Daniel remained, but she couldn't ignore the heavy toll it was taking on her emotional and mental well-being. She knew that for the sake of herself and her son, she needed to find a way to regain her strength and reclaim her identity.

She was slowly coming to the painful realization that she couldn't fix Daniel's struggles on her own, and it hurt. She had sacrificed so much of herself, hoping that her love and support would be enough to pull him out of the darkness. But now she understood that his healing journey was a battle he needed to fight within himself.

Closing the chapters of hope didn't mean giving up entirely. It meant accepting that she couldn't change Daniel or force him to confront his demons. She had to focus on preserving her own well-being and protecting Gabriel from the emotional turmoil.

As she reflected on their journey, she understood that love alone couldn't fix their problems. It would require both of them to be willing to confront their demons, to seek help, and to make the difficult choices necessary for healing and growth.

With each closed chapter of hope, Bethesda began to realize that she couldn't solely rely on the strength of her love to sustain their relationship. She needed to find her own resilience and assert her boundaries, even if it meant facing the painful truth that their relationship might not survive without both of them actively working towards a healthier future.

In her darkest moments, she allowed herself to envision a life where she could be whole again, where she could pursue her dreams without compromising her sense of self. Life ahead was uncertain and daunting, but the realization that she needed to prioritize her own well-being became a guiding light, offering promises within the shadows of despair.

As she paused at the fork of her emotions, Bethesda knew that it would require courage, self-discovery, and the willingness to let go of the likelihood that their love alone could mend their fractured relationship.

With determination, she began to take the first steps towards finding her own voice, her own strength, and the possibility of a life filled with love, happiness, and a sense of self. The chapters of her story were far from over, and she was ready to write the next ones, hoping that they would lead her towards healing and the realization of her own worth.

Within all of the chaos, Bethesda remained true to herself. She knew that she deserved better. While her heart ached for the future she had once envisioned with Daniel, she also knew that her happiness and emotional health couldn't be sacrificed for the sake of a fading dream.

CHAPTER 21

RELIGION RUINED MY LIFE

Bethesda found herself in the quiet moments of solitude, reflecting on her religious upbringing. From a young age, she was taught that her role was to be submissive and to take care of the home, mirroring the teachings she heard from the pulpit and read in the biblical scriptures. The expectations placed on her felt like shackles, constricting her potential and stifling her aspirations.

The words she had heard countless times echoed in her mind: "Woman, be silent." It was a verse she had come across in the Bible, and she had been raised to believe that it was her duty to adhere to these words. It appeared as though her voice and opinions were unimportant and that the only thing that mattered to her was how well she could help and support others, regardless of how happy and content she might be herself.

The burden of these expectations weighed heavily on her. She couldn't help but wonder how these teachings had played a part in shaping her current situation. Had her ingrained belief in submission and self-sacrifice contributed to her accepting Daniel's hurtful behavior and emotional abuse for so long?

As she contemplated her religious upbringing, she struggled with conflicting emotions. On the one hand, she cherished her faith and the comfort it brought her during challenging times. On the other hand, she felt a growing resentment towards the ways in which religion had been used to control and suppress her, perpetuating the idea that she should endure suffering for the sake of the gospel.

They went to church regularly and pretended to be the perfect Christian family. Of course, Daniel was a model of decency in the eyes of the world, a guy who commanded respect and adoration in our professional, religious, and social circles. Together, we were the couple everyone looked up to - a harmonious duo whose lives seemed like models of perfection. But behind closed doors, a separate, unpleasant reality was unfolding.

She thought about the time when the burden of striving to maintain the façade of the perfect Christian family was becoming too much for her to bear and contacted the pastor in hopes of sharing the emotional rollercoaster that had become an everyday reality and seeking wisdom. Unfortunately, the pastor found it difficult to connect Daniel's polished exterior with the turmoil she described. It seemed impossible to him that the man who seemed so active in ministry and, of course, gave finances so liberally should be the source of her anguish. His counsel directed her to prioritize supporting her husband over her own aspirations, reinforcing the idea that the primary duty of a wife was to tend to her husband's needs. After hearing his advice, she felt more constrained and alone, trapped by traditional norms and Daniel's seductive facade.

Her sense of hopelessness grew stronger over time. She had given up the position as head of the women's department, which she had once relished. Daniel had successfully persuaded her that she did not fit the image of a "church woman." He was adamant that her lack of humility and outspokenness would incite rebellion among the other women. Now she sees that his motivation was fear - fear that the hidden darkness buried within their lives would be revealed.

People in their religious community thought that she had become spiritually distant because of her heavy use of makeup, ignorant of the fact that it was her shield to hide the scars that were all over her body. There were rumors and whispers all around, but few people were brave enough to confront the hard truth. It was much easier for them to turn away and hold on to the idea that they had a perfect family than to deal with the ugly reality.

Bethesda prayed for someone to see past the mask and understand the silent agony she was going through. But cultural expectations and Daniel's charm overshadowed her pleas for help, trapping her in a nightmare reality that felt impossible to escape.

The relentless demands placed upon her by Daniel and the chaos within the congregation took a devastating toll on her emotional, physical, and mental well-being. This church, unlike her cherished home congregation, had become a place of strife and discord. Instead of a haven where people of faith came together to support one another, this community was marred by arguments, slander, and envy among its members, even within the pastoral leadership. The big difference between what they did and the ideals of love and kindness was disappointing.

Her anxiety, which she had always kept hidden, began to spiral out of control. Even when she tried to sleep, the church's constant drama and toxic environment kept her on guard, preventing her from finding serenity in her life.

In the middle of her troubles, she decided to seek comfort and help, trying to find another woman she could talk to and who would understand what she was going through. She was surprised to find out that many of those she reached out to were just as lonely and mentally worn out as she was, and those who weren't rejected her.

She suffered in silence, gradually erecting a defensive wall to protect herself from both the toxicity of the church and her husband's manipulation of religion, in which Daniel would selectively quote biblical verses out of context, using them as a weapon to justify his control over her and their relationship. He frequently reminded her of passages in the Bible that emphasized submission and obedience, which he used to silence her and undermine her feelings and opinions.

When Bethesda tried to assert herself or express her own desires, he would use religion as a means to guilt her into submission. He would tell her that as a Christian wife, she should prioritize his needs and wishes above her own and that questioning his authority was equivalent to questioning God's plan.

Bethesda, who loved the man who had turned their shared faith into a tool of power and dominance, couldn't help but feel betrayed. It was a painful realization that the person she had entrusted her heart and life to was using their religious beliefs to keep her in a state of vulnerability and subservience. She no longer had faith in him because of her mistrust and suspicion.

Despite her emotional turmoil, Bethesda recognized that Daniel's interpretation of her faith and spirituality did not define her. She began to distinguish between the true teachings and the twisted version he had imposed on her.

She knew deep down that her faith was not meant to be an oppressive tool or a justification for abuse. Through Jesus Christ, it was intended to be a source of love and compassion. This realization sparked a desire within her to rediscover her faith in a way that empowered her, allowing her to embrace her worth, reclaim her voice, and challenge the harmful interpretations of scripture that had been used to keep women in submissive roles. She read the texts with a critical eye, hoping to gain a better understanding of the message they were conveying. During her search, she came across stories in the

Bible about strong and courageous women who defied societal norms and stood up for what they believed.

These revelations opened her eyes to a new perspective, one that valued equality, love, and mutual respect in relationships. She realizes that submission does not imply giving up her life, but rather fulfilling the purpose that was assigned to her.

She sought to reconnect with her inner strength and rediscover her passions and aspirations as she questioned the teachings that had shaped her life. She refused to let false religion dictate her worth and choices any longer.

Bethesda's journey of self-discovery led her to confront the idea that religion, when taken to its logical conclusion, can be used to manipulate and control, leaving people feeling trapped and hopeless. But she also found hope in the realization that, when interpreted with love and compassion, her faith could be a source of healing and empowerment.

She knew she was on a path to breaking free from the chains of religious expectations that had held her captive for far too long as the chapters of her life continued to unfold. She was determined to rewrite her own story, one that valued her worth, dreams, and voice - a story of liberation and empowerment.

In the end, she realized that true faith and spirituality were much larger than the confines of a church. It was about finding peace, love, and kindness within oneself and showing those qualities to others, regardless of their beliefs or group affiliation. Religion, when practiced with genuine love and compassion, has the potential to be a beacon of hope for healing and self-discovery. Her newfound faith enabled her to emerge from the darkness of submission and reclaim her life with renewed strength and purpose.

CHAPTER 22

KINSUGI

Bethesda moved around the house doing her daily chores, but she was still thinking about how hard things were with Daniel and how much debt he was getting into. As she walked down the hallway, she got a quick glimpse of a scary image in a mirror. It was a face she didn't know -one that looked sad and hopeless.

She walked back the way she came, her shaky steps echoing through the empty hallways. Her heart beat hard in her chest, and she took short gasps of air. She stood in front of the mirror again and slowly raised her eyes to look at the face she didn't know.

Even though it was her own image, she felt like it was someone else's. Her pain had turned her once-bright eyes dark, and she had stopped smiling a long time ago. Her cheeks were still stained with tears, and her lips trembled with the feelings she had been hiding for far too long.

Bethesda just couldn't keep going. She couldn't handle the shock or the fact that she had changed so much that she didn't even recognize herself. She broke down in front of the mirror and cried as her shoulders shook and tears ran down her face. Her cries filled the empty house and echoed through the rooms as if she were pleading for salvation from the depths of her despair.

In that moment of weakness, she had to face the harsh fact that she was no longer herself. Her battles and sacrifices had buried the woman she used to know - the one with hopes and dreams. It was a scary discovery that made her feel a lot of emotions she hadn't felt in a long time. Bethesda contemplates the choices she has made and wonders if she could have done things differently. She longs for the strength and resilience she once possessed, the ability to face life's hurdles with grace and determination.

As the tears kept coming, Bethesda made a silent promise to rediscover the person she used to be and heal the wounds that had torn her apart. She now imagines herself as a pottery bowl that has been smashed into many pieces and strewn across the road, with each piece representing a piece of her old existence. Every day that goes by feels like another car running over her, shattering her spirit even more.

She wonders if she'll ever be able to put those broken pieces back together again. It will be like assembling a shattered ceramic bowl, it will take time, patience, and careful effort. She acknowledges that she can't do this alone and needs to find the courage to seek help, to open up to those she trusts, and to accept that, although she is afraid of what lies ahead, she can't keep living like a stranger within.

Battered, bruised, and lonely, there still remains a glimmer of light that tells her she can find her way back to the strong, vibrant woman she once was.

More determined than ever, she made up her mind not to allow her life to be defined by the shattered pieces on the highway. Instead, she will use those broken fragments as a foundation for growth and transformation. She will reclaim her identity, her dreams, and her aspirations, no longer sacrificing herself for the sake of others.

As she steps away from the mirror, Bethesda carries with her the strength to face challenges, to rebuild her life, and to embrace the journey of self-discovery and healing. In the midst of adversity, she has found her wake-up moment, and with it, the determination to rise stronger and shine brighter than ever before.

In her quest for healing and self-discovery, Bethesda stumbled upon the ancient Japanese art of kintsugi, which is the practice of repairing broken pottery with gold or silver lacquer. The philosophy behind this technique resonated deeply with her - it celebrated the beauty of imperfection and embraced the idea that something broken could be transformed into something even more valuable and precious.

Making a decision to apply the kintsugi technique to her own life, she used it as a metaphor to represent the process of picking up the shattered pieces of her discouragement, emptiness, low self-esteem, and loneliness. She started by admitting that she was broken inside and that life had left her with scars and wounds . She didn't didn't try to hide them or act like they didn't exist. Instead, she made them a part of her story.

Using self-compassion and self-love as the "gold lacquer," Bethesda began to put the broken pieces back together. She let herself feel the pain, sadness, and anger she had been holding for a long time and worked through them. As she put the golden seal on each crack in her heart, she understood that these hard times had made her a strong, caring person.

Through therapy and thinking about herself, Bethesda started to figure out why she felt lonely and had low self-esteem. She understood that trying to get approval from other people made her feel empty and that she needed to learn how to find satisfaction within herself.

With each step she took on her way to getting better, she found new skills and interests. She got back into drawing and writing, which let her show how she felt and what she had been through.

As Bethesda continued to follow the kintsugi mindset, it helped her to talk to other people who had been through similar things. She surrounded herself with friends and family who understood and loved her no matter what.

Over time, the cracks in her heart became less painful memories of the past and more signs of her growth and change. She understood that the gold lacquer she used to fix herself wasn't just a layer on the outside; it also exhibited how strong and wise she had become on the inside.

Bethesda found a sense of purpose and reality as she picked up the bits of her life and put them back together with the golden glue of self-compassion and self-love. She embraced her imperfections and realized that this was what made her unique and beautiful.

With kintsugi's beautiful touch on her heart, Bethesda no longer saw herself as broken. Instead, she saw herself as a work of art - a masterpiece in progress, who learned that healing was not about erasing the scars but embracing them as part of herself.

She carried the wisdom of kintsugi with her as a reminder that she was stronger and more useful than she had ever been. The practice of picking up her broken pieces had led her to a place of empowerment and self-discovery, where she could finally shine brightly in her own light.

VOICES OF WOMEN

In the swirling chaos of New York City, I was a beacon of dedication and commitment, both to my family and my work. I didn't believe in the notion of divorce, or at least I hadn't. It wasn't what I envisioned for myself or what I tried to cultivate in my marriage.

I was that ideal partner who left no stone unturned. In our home, the aroma of his favorite dishes, which, for the record, were more sophisticated than mere grilled cheese sandwiches, filled the air. The floors gleamed, and the laundry was either neatly folded or left in the capable hands of the launderers. And this wasn't all leisure; my days were long and arduous, serving patrons at the post office six days a week.

Weekends? They weren't for rest. My voice, a siren's call, serenaded audiences at various events, both within the city's buzzing boundaries and beyond. There was no pause. Even when I was providing round-the-clock care at the hospice, I would come back home, the journey interspersed only by two-week intervals.

I also owned a moving company, a testament to my entrepreneurial spirit. I was hands-on, managing the operations until my pregnancy progressed to its third trimester.

And even when I momentarily stepped away from work, my feet never really settled. While searching for a new apartment and navigating the labyrinthine streets of the city on foot or through its intricate web of public transport, I was perpetually in motion.

But hidden beneath these layers of responsibilities and actions was a sinister shadow that plagued my life. I navigated a treacherous minefield of physical, mental, and emotional abuse. Although, to the outside world we were the epitome of harmony — a happy couple, but behind closed doors, the threat to my very existence loomed large.

Night after restless night, sleep eluded me, held at bay by the palpable fear that it might be my last. His preferred method of terror was to suffocate the very life out of me, his fingers tightening around my throat. And as if the external torments weren't enough, relentless migraines bore into my skull, an unyielding reminder of the pain both outside and inside.

My husband was cocooned in all the luxuries and affections I could provide. From the intimate whispers of our bedroom to shielding him from the world's prying eyes and making justifications where none were needed, I gave it my all. If love could take a tangible form, my face, worn yet content, would personify it.

But over time, the relentless giving and endless sacrifices took a toll. I gave so much that I no longer recognised myself and felt lost, having strayed far from the essence of who I truly was.

As Bethesda lost herself, I did likewise and had to come to a decision whether to remain in this relationship or walk. But thanks to my Heavenly Father, who kept me throughout this horrible ordeal and gave me the courage to make the right choice, I was able to pick up the broken pieces and become whole again.

Erica

CHAPTER 23

THE CROSSROADS OF CHOICE

Bethesda stood at a pivotal point in her life, torn between two paths that lay ahead of her. Years of enduring a deteriorating marriage with Daniel had led her to this moment of decision. As she reflected on the struggles, the pain, and the shattered pieces of her heart, she knew that she had reached a crossroad.

Leaving was a frightening option, but it offered the possibility of freedom from the misery that had consumed her for far too long. It was a chance for restoration—a fresh start in a life that she had longed for. The thought of breaking free from the suffocating grip of a toxic relationship provided optimism for her future.

She couldn't, however, ignore the influence it would have on Gabriel, who had already been through a lot in his young life and would now have to adjust to a one-parent family. She worries about how this transformation will impact him and how it could affect his ideas of love and relationships. If she does make this decision, she will ensure that his paternal grandparents remain an active part of his life.

Staying, on the other hand, meant committing to a life of uncertainty in which Daniel's harmful conduct went uncontrolled. The idea that things might stay the same or even get worse was a big worry for her. Could she handle more years of sadness and mental turmoil that caused her to shatter?

As Bethesda thought about her options, she looked inside herself for help. She knew she was worthy of being loved, respected, and happy. She deserved to live a life where she could shine brightly, away from Daniel's anger and control. But it wasn't easy to make such a life-altering decision. It meant she would have to face her fears, the unknown, and the idea of starting over. It meant realizing that her worth wasn't defined by Daniel's actions but by her own strength and resilience.

After living under the strong control of Daniel's decision-making for her, Bethesda finally recognizes that she doesn't need permission from anyone to make the choices she desires. She has spent years second-guessing herself and seeking approval from others, especially Daniel, but now she understands that her happiness and well-being is in her own hands.

Bethesda began to take small steps toward reclaiming her independence by seeking counseling to address the trauma from years of emotional and physical abuse as she sat in the cozy office of her therapist, holding on to a tissue as if it were her last hope. She had been going to therapy for a few weeks, and today was the day she was ready to face the hardest part of her marriage.

"Take your time, Bethesda," her therapist, Dr. Anderson, told her softly.

Bethesda took a shaky breath and spoke with a trembling voice: "It's... it's the way he made me feel small and useless. How he used words as tools to hurt me until I felt like I had no value at all."

As she talked, Daniel's hurtful words and deeds kept coming back to her mind. The therapist listened carefully and gave her a safe place to talk about the heavy things that had been bothering her for years. Bethesda felt angry and sad at the same time. As she talked about the mental and physical abuse she had been through, tears ran down her face.

Dr. Anderson nodded sympathetically and agreed that Bethesda had been through a lot of pain. "I'm so sorry, Bethesda, that you had to go through that. It's important to remember that you didn't do anything wrong."

Feeling supported, Bethesda started to talk about how she had decided to go to therapy and start taking steps to get her freedom back. She talked about her fears, how self-doubt had held her prisoner, and how she had finally realized she deserved better.

"Therapy has given me a lifeline," Bethesda said, her voice now steadier. I'm learning to recognize the patterns of control and manipulation to which I've become so accustomed ~~to~~. I'm starting to break free from their grasp."

Dr. Anderson gave Bethesda a thumbs-up and said, "That's a big step. It takes time to get your freedom and sense of self-worth back, but you're on the right track."

As the therapy meetings went on, Bethesda started to feel better about herself and find out who she was. She found the power in herself that she had been ignoring for a long time. With Dr. Anderson's help, she learned to set limits, spot harmful habits, and speak up for her own needs and wants.

Slowly but surely, Bethesda started to heal. She realized that she was not defined by the scars of her past and that she had the power to create a brighter future for herself. Each session brought her closer to the person she used to be - the one who had hopes and goals and was determined to live a life free from abuse and full of self-love and independence.

On one visit, Bethesda confided in her therapist that although Daniel's parents had informed her that he had a mental disorder, she could not get rid of the impression that something deeper and more significant was being kept hidden.

The therapist, who conveyed calm and empathy, listened closely to her worries.

"I understand how frustrating it can be when you feel like there's something left unsaid," the therapist added, smiling reassuringly. "When you're ready and feel comfortable, you might think about paying a visit to his parents and asking them more questions."

Bethesda nodded thoughtfully and gave a sigh of relief. She knew that asking Daniel's parents for more information could give her the piece of the puzzle that was still missing. It will be a key part of her full healing.

Despite being miles away, the love and support from her friends and family, who remained by her side throughout, assuring her that she wasn't alone and that she had the power to choose her destiny, awakened her confidence to fly back home to visit her in-laws. She decided to take Gabriel along to allow him to spend time with family and friends he hadn't seen in years.

After leaving Gabriel in the care of her parents, Bethesda embarked on a slow drive down the narrow, winding road leading to her in-laws' house. The familiar route brought back memories of the very first time she had made this journey. Back then, she believed that her visit could somehow solve the problems in her marriage, but instead, it caused them to escalate.

The burden of those previous expectations pressed against her as she navigated the same twists and turns. But things were different this time. Her goal had changed. She wasn't just trying to help Daniel and his situation anymore. This visit was exactly what she needed for herself. It was a step toward realizing how complicated their relationship was and finding closure.

Bethesda whispered a prayer for a good result, hoping and feeling uncertain at the same time. She hoped that this visit, which was meant to help her heal and understand herself, would go well and let her start a new part of her life.

Emotions overflowed as Bethesda stepped into her in-laws' warm embrace. Hugs and kisses spoke volumes, a silent testament to the depth of their love and concern. They had a sense of why she had made this special trip, and they didn't prolong the process of opening up to her. Their eyes were heavy with years of unspoken truth, and they felt the weight of the secrets they were about to reveal.

Apologies tumbled from their lips as they expressed remorse for not sharing the entire story with her before. Their voices quivered with a mixture of guilt and hope, and they spoke in halting breaths.

"We're sorry, Bethesda," they began, their words hanging in the air like a fragile promise. "We didn't tell you everything, but we thought you might have been able to help him.

"Bethesda sat across from Daniel's mother, a gentle flicker of candlelight casting shadows on the room's worn wooden furniture. They had shared a previous conversation in this cozy space, but tonight was different. There was an air of solemnity that hung between them, a weighty secret that needed to be revealed.

With a deep sigh, Daniel's mother began, her voice trembling slightly, "Bethesda, I need to tell you something, something I've kept hidden for far too long. It's about Daniel, about why he is the way he is."

Bethesda's eyes locked onto hers, her face a mixture of concern and curiosity. "I'm here for you, whatever it is," she assured her.

His mother nodded, her eyes glistening with tears that had long been held back. "His mental problems run deep, but they're not his fault. It's the result of something else, something that happened many years ago."

She took a moment to gather her thoughts before continuing, her voice heavy with emotion. "It all started with me, Bethesda. I was looking for my husband one day, and I went to church—the very church where we've worshipped all our lives. He was a part of the ministral staff, a man we both trusted and respected."

Bethesda listened intently, her brow wrinkling as she sensed the seriousness of the revelation.

"On that day," Daniel's mother continued, "he betrayed that trust in the most horrifying way possible. He assaulted me, Bethesda, in the house of God."

Bethesda gasped, her hand instinctively covering her mouth. She couldn't imagine the pain and trauma that Daniel's mother had endured.

"I confided in my husband," she went on, "and together, we made a terrible decision. We chose to keep it a secret to protect the church and ourselves from shame and judgment."

Her voice grew even softer as she revealed the next agonizing part of the story. "But our darkest moment was yet to come. I became pregnant as a result of that dreadful day, and I didn't want to keep the child. What were we supposed to do? Our faith, Bethesda, didn't allow for abortion. It was considered murder."

Tears rose in her eyes as she continued to recount the painful past. "So, we decided that I would have the child and that we would put him up for adoption. To make it happen without anyone discovering the truth, we moved far away to a place where no one knew us."

Bethesda's heart ached for the woman before her, a mother who had endured such unspeakable pain. She reached out and placed a comforting hand on her shoulder.

"Throughout my pregnancy," Daniel's mother whispered, "I lived in isolation, cut off from the world. I had no attachment to the child growing inside me. I left everything up to my husband to handle the adoption process. I was ready to give him up and continue with my life."

A sob escaped her lips as she continued, "But after the child was born, my husband couldn't bear to part with him. He wanted a son so badly, Bethesda, and he couldn't let him go, not even for the sake of our secret."

Bethesda listened in stunned silence, her heart heavy with the weight of the revelation.

Daniel's mother wiped away her tears and concluded, "And so, we kept him, despite the torment it brought me daily. I never had a motherly bond with him, but by God's grace, I was able to love him at a distance."

She took a deep breath, and her eyes filled with a mixture of relief and anguish. "Daniel doesn't know any of this, and we would appreciate it if you didn't share it with him."

Bethesda nodded, her own heart aching for both Daniel and his mother. She recognized the depth of her husband's ignorance about his own roots as she absorbed the heartbreaking story. The web of lies, secrets, and sorrow had shaped his life in ways he never could have imagined. The truth had been laid bare—a secret that had been carried for far too long, and it was a heavy burden they now shared.

At the crossroads of choice, Bethesda found her voice and her strength to gain clarity on what she truly wanted for her future. And with that knowledge, she took a deep breath and embraced the power to shape her own destiny, one step at a time.

CHAPTER 24

SHINING MY DESTINY

Seven years had passed since Bethesda began her journey of healing and self-rediscovery. Each sunrise had etched lessons of pain, growth, and triumph on her soul. Now, as she took a moment before the stage's beckoning lights, she was moved almost to tears looking into the mirror. The eyes that gazed back were luminous, echoing tales of strength, confidence, and hard-won resilience. No longer did she see a fragmented reflection, but a woman healed and whole, a living testament to the enduring spirit of the human heart.

The road she walked had been arduous, each step demanding the shedding of burdensome layers of pain and self-doubt. It was as if, through every tear shed, every whispered self-affirmation in the dark, she was unearthing the true Bethesda - a woman of innate beauty and unyielding strength.

With a deep breath, she stepped onto the stage. The spotlight warmed her skin, but it was the sea of eager eyes, the hushed anticipation of young women awaiting her story, that truly touched her. Her energy - vibrant and magnetic - pulled them in, weaving a bond of shared understanding and hope. With every word, with every gesture, she wore her newfound self-belief like a radiant mantle. This woman before them wasn't a victim of her past; she was its master, a beacon of love, power, and positive transformation.

While recounting her darkest moments, her voice quivered with raw emotion rather than fear. She trembles in fear whenever anyone she knows from her church, the grocery store, or even her own neighborhood catch a glimpse of the eerie scars that have disfigured her flesh. The fleeting pity or discomfort in their gaze would often cause them to look away. Those short moments, so full of unsaid words, served as savage flashbacks to her turbulent history. But they also gave her the motivation to rise above.

Bethesda's message, pulsing with heartfelt emotion, was an anthem of hope and empowerment. It was a gentle whisper to every soul: "Find yourself, love yourself." She urged her listeners to break free from the cruel shackles of societal judgments and the torment of self-doubt. With an impassioned plea, she spoke of the sacredness of self-love and self-care, urging her audience to prioritize their mental and emotional well-being.

Every word Bethesda uttered radiated with passion and sincerity, deeply resonating with her audience. By revealing her struggles, she inspired others to face their own challenges and initiate their healing journeys.

Bethesda's life had been a horrific rollercoaster ride. Yet, she had emerged resilient and unyielding. As a symbol of her journey, she held up a distinctive bracelet crafted from an old, discolored pair of jeans that had gone through many years of wear and tear. The bracelet, made of seemingly discarded fragments, of her life, ripped into pieces that seemed of no use anymore. Yet, she had transformed what some would consider garbage into something beautiful.

Her eyes met those of the young ladies, filled with determination and hope. She wanted them to understand that just like the bracelet, their lives might have experienced challenges and hardships, but those very experiences could be transformed into something extraordinary.

"Look at this bracelet," she began, with a warm resonated voice, "and remember that life's trials and struggles don't define who you are," "Like these old jeans, we all go through times of wear and tear, but those experiences can be the very threads that weave together a beautiful tapestry of strength and resilience."

As she spoke, the young ladies leaned in, captivated by her words and the symbolism of the bracelet. They listened intently, recognizing in Bethesda's journey a reflection of their own struggles and uncertainties.

"I, too, have faced moments of doubt and darkness," she continued, "But just like this bracelet, I chose to gather the fragmented pieces of my life and weave them back together with threads of hope, love, and self-acceptance."

Bethesda's vulnerability created a safe space for them open up and share their own stories. She encouraged them to see the beauty within themselves, even in the face of challenges and mistakes.

"You are not defined by your past or the struggles you face," Bethesda reminded them, her voice firm but compassionate. "You have the power to embrace your unique journey and create something extraordinary out of the seemingly ordinary pieces of your life."

"Remember, just as God's plan worked through imperfect hearts in the past, it can shape a beautiful future through your imperfections too."

The room was filled with a sense of empowerment and possibility. They were inspired to reflect on their own lives, acknowledging that they, too, could create something beautiful from the challenges they had faced.

As Bethesda concluded her talk, the young ladies erupted into applause, their hearts touched by her authenticity and the message she had shared. She believe that each of them had a new reality of hope and determination, ready to face their journeys with courage and self-love. Before leaving, each one received a Bethesda bracelet kit to create and have as a tangible reminder of the power within them to transform their lives.

Her mission to empower these young ladies had just begun. Through her movement, "Radiate Your Purpose," she would continue to be a guiding light, reminding them that they had the strength and resilience to turn their struggles into stepping stones towards a brighter and more beautiful future. With her movement, she was determined to continue spreading hope and empowering them to embrace their destinies, no matter the challenges they faced and shine brightly in a world that had once felt dim.

Bethesda's path had led her to this point, where she was making a difference in the lives of these young hearts, and she felt a sense of fulfillment and purpose that was overpowering. Her journey had been one of change, and she had emerged not just as a survivor but also as someone who was no longer defined by her past or bound by the shadows that had formerly tormented her. Bethesda saw that she had become a symbol of courage and inspiration, living proof that one could "Rise Strong and Shine Bright" despite the fragments life had dealt them.

Walking off of the stage she looks back and hear the silence that now overtakes the auditorium that once was filled with all types of emotions. Her assistant gathers her belongings and joins her as they proceed toward the parking lot. In the shadow of the night a young lady begin to walk toward them. As she gets closer, Bethesda can see that she is overwhelmed with tears streaming down her flushed cheeks. Their eyes met and Bethesda gave her a warm hug that spoke volumes without saying a word.

She watched as the young lady walked away.......

About the Author

BERNICE BROWN, affectionately dubbed "D'Author" by her adoring granddaughter, is more than just a name in the world of literature. She is a mentor, author, an inspiring speaker with a passion for helping women "Shine Their Destiny." With a heart full of compassion and a voice resonating with hope, she motivates them to surmount adversity, breathe life back into their dormant dreams, and ignite the inner spark to attain those dreams. Bernice stands firm in her conviction that every woman has extraordinary inner strength. Anchored in the belief that nothing in life is mere happenstance, she asserts that every twist and turn, every challenge and triumph, is a part of a greater purpose. She passionately urges women: Don't allow adversities to bind their spirit, and now is the moment to reclaim their dreams and radiate brilliance.

www.iamlavandared.com

Acknowledgments

To Brenda, Monica, Sherri, Susie, Claressa, Danna, Erica, and Nora,

The journey of creating "Rise Strong~Shine Bright" has been a deeply transformative one, and it would not have been possible without each of your invaluable contributions.

Every book is not just a solitary endeavor but a collective effort, a harmonious convergence of voices, ideas, and passions. Each one of you has added a unique note to this symphony, pouring your insights, wisdom, and experience into every word.

It is my heartfelt belief that the stories we tell and the wisdom we share have the power to create waves of change. Your words, so generously shared, are set to ripple out and touch the hearts of countless women, offering guidance, comfort, and inspiration.

I want to express my sincere gratitude for believing in this process, for being a symbol of strength and vulnerability, and for making sure that your words will have an eternal impact on the lives of many women.

Thank you for making "Rise Strong~Shine Bright" not just a book but a luminous testament to the strength, resilience, and brilliance of women everywhere.

With utmost appreciation,

Bernice~

Dear Strong and Resilient Women,

Life sometimes places us in situations where we are tested beyond what we could have ever imagined. It can feel as though you're the only one going through this ordeal. Please understand that you are not alone. Many women have overcome seemingly insurmountable obstacles to become even stronger and more resilient. Your journey, while uniquely yours, resonates with the stories of many before you.

Believe in your Creator, who has given you the fortitude and strength to overcome. When the weight gets too heavy, draw on others around you for support, direction, and a listening ear— friends, family, or experts. Remember that setting boundaries is perfectly acceptable. It is acceptable to say no.

You are not defined by this moment or situation but by the vast tapestry of experiences, dreams, aspirations, and the love you carry within you.

You are not just a survivor, but a warrior. With every challenge you face, you're writing a narrative of resilience and hope. Never doubt your worth or the strength you possess and know that brighter days are ahead.

Remember, even in the toughest moments, your strength is immeasurable, and your worth is invaluable.

I'm sending you my love, strength, and unyielding support.

Bernice~

Made in the USA
Middletown, DE
30 October 2023

41635658R00116